KRISTA'S VEXATION

GEMMA JACKSON

POOLBEG

Also by Gemma Jackson

Through Streets Broad and Narrow
Ha'penny Chance
The Ha'penny Place
Ha'penny Schemes
Impossible Dream
Dare to Dream
Her Revolution
Cherish the Dream

THE *KRISTA* SERIES OF NOVELLAS

Krista's Escape
Krista's Journey
Krista's Choice
Krista's Chance
Krista's Dilemma
Krista's Doubt
Krista's Duty
Krista's Deeds

Published by Poolbeg

Published 2023

by Poolbeg Press Ltd.

123 Grange Hill, Baldoyle,

Dublin 13, Ireland

Email: poolbeg@poolbeg.com

A catalogue record for this book is available from the British Library.

ISBN 978178199-512-9

www.poolbeg.com

PREFACE

Dear Reader,

Welcome back to Krista's world! I've had a great deal of fun researching this period in history. I've learnt a great deal. But, as I have said before, I am not writing a history book. I seek to entertain.

In this book I write about the Wrens giggling, weeping and generally carrying on. I based the reaction on my time in Belgium. I had to register at the local police station. Therefore, the police knew there was a French-speaking Irish person in the district. As a result, I was awoken time without number to translate for young women who had got themselves into trouble through their innocence and ignorance. I wanted to write to their families and read them the riot act for allowing young women to leave all-girl schools and travel out into the world. They hadn't a bull's notion of how to behave and protect themselves. The Belgian police would shake their heads in disbelief when I tried to explain how they thought the person offering them somewhere to live for free "was such a nice man".

I also did a great deal of research on guns. Imagine, living in Northern Ireland and conducting in-depth research on guns – I hope the police are not at my door someday soon to find out what is going on.

I was astonished to discover that the Enfield handgun that the forces used looks exactly like the six-shooter guns that cowboys use in the movies. Honestly, check it out. I had to check more than once just to be sure. I was tempted to make Krista a sharpshooter, but I refrained – with difficulty.

Some of the research I conduct for these books can be very frustrating. I find mention of something – follow the clues – then lose the scent. So much of what happened to the women in the forces is still shrouded in mystery.

I have taken some liberties with what is known but then – I am writing fiction.

I hope you enjoy this latest episode in *Krista's War*.

Gemma

CHAPTER 1

December 4th

1939

Near Dover, Kent

Krista Lestrange, her white-blonde hair flattened beneath the uniform hat pulled low over her brow, didn't care how ridiculous she might look. She was performing jumping jacks, her tall, elegant body hidden in the cold, wet, dark evening. She hoped the bus she was waiting for arrived before she froze solid. The chill of the evening breeze was cutting through her clothing and practically freezing her to the marrow.

That morning she had left their cottage in the company of her fellow Wrens Elaine Greenwood and Eugenie Carpenter, wearing her full dress uniform with skirt and thick lisle stockings. Her friend Peregrine Fotheringham-Carter had slept on the sofa in their cottage last night. This morning he offered to drive the three Wrens to headquarters based in nearby Dover Castle. The three women would normally ride their motorcycles to the castle but today all three Wrens had been tasked to report to the powers that be. That required full dress uniform – not ideal for riding motorcycles through wet streets. They were to report on their findings and opinions concerning a prototype heavy-goods vehicle that had been converted for use as a campervan – an army and navy joint project. Perry and the Wrens had previously camped in it, before travelling from Norfolk to Dover in the relative comfort of the large vehicle. Their motorcycles had been stored securely inside the prototype vehicle, saving the Wrens the long motorcycle journey back to base.

She heard the sound of an engine and almost groaned aloud in relief. How on earth would the driver be able to tell that there was someone waiting at the dark bus stop? She did not dare step out into the road. One read about accidents that occurred in the dark of night, now that all streetlights had been extinguished by order of the War Office. She walked to the rim of the kerb, took her hat from her head and waved it up and down, praying she would attract the bus driver's attention. The sound of brakes being applied and the greatly reduced beam of the bus headlamps appearing out of the darkness almost brought tears to her eyes. The War Office demanded that all vehicle light emissions be reduced but the twin narrow beams of light were a blissful sight on this cold, damp, dark night.

"Mind how you step there, missus!" The bus conductor leaned out the opening door to shout.

Krista grasped the silver bar and pulled herself up onto the bus. The friendly conductor followed in her footsteps while the bus pulled away from the stop. It was difficult to see but, after spending so long in the black of night, Krista was able to make out a vacant seat and gratefully sat down. She held out the threepenny piece she had borrowed from Vicky Nixon, a Wren she knew from their time together at a London secretarial school.

She then gave the general location of the bus stop nearest to her rented cottage.

"You one of Mrs Fagin's girls?" The bus conductor took her money, tapped on the silver metal ticket-machine hanging from his neck onto his chest, dropped her money into the leather moneybag hanging down to his hip. He passed her ticket and the change into her open hand.

"Yes, Mrs Fagin is my landlady." Krista was relieved that he appeared to recognise the address she had given him. "Can you please tell me when we are approaching the stop?" She knew where the bus stop was, of course – Gerda Mueller, a Wren who had shared the cottage with them, had taken the bus daily – but this was the first time Krista had used the service and she was unsure of her bearings in the dark.

"I can do that, doll."

"You been going to the picture house again, Bert?" a female voice called, the speaker an indistinguishable blob in the darkness. "You sound like one of them gangsters from the pictures my old man likes so much."

"Now, now, Mrs Hartley, I mean no offence," the conductor replied good-naturedly.

"I know Mrs Fagin," said the woman, "and if you forget to tell the young woman where to get off, I'll give her a shout. Never you mind, young miss. We won't let you pass your stop in the dark."

There was a mumble of agreement from other passengers.

"Thank you!" Krista called out.

"I'll give you a shout when we get close," the conductor said, walking away.

Krista sat back with a sigh. It was not a long bus journey from Dover Castle to the cottage the navy rented from Mrs Fagin. She had no idea how long the journey would take with the driver forced to drive slowly and carefully down dark country lanes.

She was aware of the muted conversations taking place around her from her fellow passengers. There was no point trying to look out the window. She was left with her own thoughts for company.

The day had started out with such promise. The three Wrens – Strange, Green and Wood – and Perry had prepared breakfast with the foods left for them by Mrs. Fagin. They had laughed and wondered about the upcoming meeting with the heads of the different services. Krista had her shorthand notebooks filled with their impressions of the prototype campervan close to hand. She'd planned to type up the notes later before attending the meeting. With a great deal of laughter and good cheer, they had prepared for the day ahead.

A hand on her shoulder startled her.

"This is your stop, flower."

A woman stood at her shoulder, a group of people at her back.

"We're all getting off here – be careful how you step. How we're expected to see where we're going when you can't see your hand in front of your face, I do not know – still, mustn't grumble."

The cottage was in darkness. Was it possible she was the first back? Krista opened the gate into the garden and shuffled her way forward, afraid to lift her feet in case she stumbled. She reached the door without mishap, pushed the letterbox open and felt with her cold fingers for the string that hung from the letterbox down to the floor with a key attached. She pulled the string up and out, and used the key to open the door.

Once inside with the door closed, she pulled the blackout curtain over the glass of the entry door. Her hands slapped the wall, seeking the light switch. She wanted to fall to her knees in gratitude for the light beaming from a bare electric bulb.

She hurried around the downstairs rooms, pulling blackout curtains over every window. In the kitchen, she opened the door in the range.

"I don't know which of you Fagin females cleaned the grate and set the fire but thank you! Thank you from the bottom of my heart." She put one of the long matches she pulled from the range mantel to the crumpled papers, sticks and black nuggets of coal packed into the range fire. She repeated her actions with the sitting-room fire before rushing upstairs.

"I am so cold." Her teeth were chattering. She wanted to pull her clothing from her and throw it on the floor but resisted the temptation – she had only one tailored dress uniform. She put her hat on a shelf, her jacket and skirt on a hanger, untied the laces of her shoes and kicked them onto the floor of the wardrobe. A shiver shook her body while she pushed her garter belt and stockings down her legs.

"I could have used a pair of the Wren uniform passion-killer navy knickers tonight. The wind whistling up my legs and under my skirt ..." She pushed her legs into her brown tweed slacks, shivering when the satin lining touched her naked skin. She pulled on a green knitted twinset and, with socks and a pair of fur-lined slippers on her feet, ran down the stairs and into the kitchen.

She huddled before the open door of the range with her hands held out towards the cheerily flaming fire. She rubbed her hands together checking the kitchen surfaces with her eyes. Mrs Fagin left food for what she called "her Wrens" to heat up. She found what she was looking for in the pantry: a large pot of stew sitting on a slate slab to keep fresh. She carried the pot to the range and put it on the back where it could slowly heat. With a ladle she scooped stew into a smaller pot she put on the free-standing gas stove top to heat for her own meal. While she waited for the stew to heat, she took a loaf of bread, a slab of butter and cheese out of the pantry. Keeping a careful eye on the smaller pot of stew, she set the table for her meal.

Elaine Greenwood pushed open the cottage door. "*Krista, where did you disappear to?*" She knew by the light peeking from around the sitting-room door that her fellow Special Wren was at home. Without waiting for a reply to her shouted comment she ran straight up the stairs.

"Be a pal, Krista." Eugenie Carpenter followed closely on Elaine's heels. "Put the kettle on! I could murder a cup of tea!"

Krista was glad her fellow Wrens were home. She pushed herself out of the comfortable armchair she'd pulled close to the sitting-room fire. She put more coal on the fire and the wire fire-screen in place before leaving the room, pulling the door tightly closed at her back to ensure the heat remained in the room.

"*Are you two hungry?*" she shouted from the bottom of the stairs.

"*Famished!*" was shouted back in two voices.

Krista hurried into the kitchen. She washed her hands at the kitchen sink before pulling the stew pot from the back of the range towards the high heat over the fire. She filled the kettle and put it on the gas stove. She set the table and cut thick slices of bread, listening to her friends shouting complaints about the cold and dark back and forth as they changed clothes.

"Where did you disappear to?" Elaine demanded as she stepped into the kitchen. She was wearing a black-and-white slacks and twinset outfit, her black hair held back from her face by a white hairband. Her blue eyes sparkled in her pretty face as she waited for Krista to answer her question.

"Me?" Krista turned from the range where she was stirring the stew. A pot of tea sat brewing on the range top. "I like that! You were the one who went off without a backward glance with your father the ship's captain."

"Krista is right." Eugenie, wearing dark-blue slacks and a pale-blue jumper, had pushed open the kitchen door. Her tiny frame, white wisps of flyaway hair and big brown eyes gave her an otherworldly appearance. Her appearance was deceptive. She was a champion three-day eventer jockey and her tiny frame was all long muscles. "We went about our business with not a thought to where she was." Because of her claustrophobia, she had been relieved to get out of the tunnels and had given no thought to anyone else. The white-washed tunnels dug deep into the cliffs and under Dover castle. She shivered to think that those tunnels would be used as a secret navy base. How could people work in the bowels of the earth?

"Have you two been together all day?" Krista began to ladle the stew into bowls.

"I spent the day with my father," Elaine said. "We don't often get time together so I'm afraid I gave no thought to anything or anyone else." She accepted a bowl of stew from Krista.

"I visited the Wrennery and had a marvellous time catching up with some of the Wrens from our training days." Eugenie took her bowl of stew from Krista before taking a seat at the kitchen table. "Did you two know that the navy supplies a ferry service – well, it's a lorry, but you know the navy – they call it a ferry." She spooned up stew and swallowed before saying, "It takes the Wrens from the castle to the Wrennery every hour on the hour."

"I learned about the ferry this evening," Krista said. "When every Wren seemed to disappear, and I was alone in the offices set aside for the Wrens' use, I saw a notice about it." She didn't want to go into detail about how alone and out of place she had felt walking the grounds of the castle. Even wearing her Special Services Wren braiding on the sleeves of her dress uniform and hat, she had been denied entrance to the tunnels. "Mr Churchill, our First Lord of the Admiralty, was in the tunnels so security was increased dramatically and I was not allowed to re-enter them. I couldn't consult Reggie, so I made my way back to the cottage. I took the bus."

"According to the discussions taking place while my father was visiting with some of his fellow ship's captains," Elaine looked at her two friends, "our navy is trying to hunt down the German armoured ship, the *Admiral Graf Spee*. The problem it's causing in the South Atlantic Ocean, sinking our merchant ships, cannot be allowed to continue unchallenged. The Germans are to be commended, of course, for evacuating the sailors before sinking our ships. Churchill would have wanted to be in the tunnels to hear reports from our ships in the South Atlantic."

"The newspapers and wireless news reports have been full of stories about the 'pocket-battleship' *Admiral Graf Spee* and the merchant ships it has sunk." Krista was not eating but had joined her friends at the kitchen table. "The British public are impressed by the fact that the *Admiral Graf Spee*'s commander allowed the crew of the *Clement* to abandon ship in its lifeboats and they safely reached Brazil. He even sent out a distress signal to ensure they were rescued. But I cannot imagine that Hitler will continue to observe such gentlemanly rules of engagement. We are at war. It is a time of savagery not gentlemanly actions." She felt the English needed to know the horrors they faced. While living in the French border town of Metz, close to the German border, she had been forced to watch the horrific changes in people she had known all her life. Everyone in Metz, it had appeared to her, lived in dread and fear while never speaking of the changes in their world. She had been thankful to escape.

"I am afraid my father agrees with Krista," Elaine almost whispered. "He doesn't believe Herr Hitler will obey the 'rules of engagement'. This is only the beginning."

"It doesn't bear thinking about." Eugenie shook her head sadly.

There was a brief silence, the women not knowing quite what to say.

"Let us change the subject. I don't mean to be hard-hearted but there is nothing we can do but hope and pray about the situation at sea." Krista stood to pour a cup of tea for herself. "Tell me, how did you two get home?"

"My father arranged a car for us." Elaine was happy to change the subject. It was enough to give one indigestion. She kept her eyes on her stew bowl, feeling guilty that they had left Krista to her own devices.

"We have rather got into the habit of going our own way," Eugenie said. "I never gave a thought to your difficulty getting back to the cottage, Krista."

"Today was an eye-opener for me." Krista sipped her tea. "I have become spoiled in having my motorcycle available to me when I wish to travel anywhere. It was quite the shock to find myself stranded, alone and penniless, at the castle. And I was so cold! I made some plans while I waited for the bus. Perhaps it is something you should both think about? I plan to buy a navy leather shoulder bag and have it with me when in dress uniform. We need to be supplied with overcoats. Our dress uniform jacket is simply not warm enough for standing outside in winter weather. Then to add insult to injury I had to borrow money from my friend Vicky for the bus back to here."

"I don't believe the factories have produced a Wren overcoat yet." Eugenie stood with her bowl in hand and ladled more stew.

"I don't care!" Krista snapped. "If all else fails I will wear my own navy coat over my uniform."

"You are in a right mood," Elaine said. "Something other than being stranded has your panties in a wad."

"Don't you mean knickers in a twist?" Eugenie laughed.

"I was trying to be polite," Elaine replied.

"Reggie was in meetings with the powers that be all day." Krista ignored their banter. "They may well still be talking as far as I know." She waited while Elaine too refilled her bowl. When everyone was back around the table she continued. "I felt like a lost lamb without plan or direction. It is not a feeling I enjoy. You two left and I was a tag-a-long with what I am coming to think of as the real Wrens. Reggie ordered me to have the events of the initial meeting in the tunnels typed up and waiting for him in his new office area." She did not discuss what had taken place inside the tunnels. It was not her place. If Reggie wanted these two to know he could tell them. "I carried out his orders but, when I returned to that building sitting apart from the main castle with the reports in hand, I had second thoughts. I refused to leave official documents in an unlocked area. If I was wrong Reggie can shout at me, but I stand by my decision. I took the reports and the one I typed up concerning our opinion on the large prototype campervan back to the security office and had them placed in a safe."

"And so you should have." Eugenie nodded. "That area set aside for our use is open to anyone at the moment. What was Reggie thinking of?"

"I don't believe he was thinking at all. He simply wanted to get the Wrens, Andorra and me out of the tunnels." Krista shrugged.

"Andorra Prendergast was there?" Eugenie gasped. "What on earth was she doing?"

"Wren First Officer Andorra Prendergast was serving coffee," Krista answered, her bright blue eyes gleaming with amusement.

"Well, I have heard everything now!" Elaine whispered.

The three sat around the kitchen table giggling at the image of the elegant upper-class woman they had trained with in Portsmouth acting as waitress.

CHAPTER 2

The shrill peal of the telephone woke the residents of the cottage in the early hours of the morning. Krista, always first to wake, fell out of her comfortable nest of blankets with a yelp. She pushed her feet into the slippers she kept by the side of her bed. She grabbed a blanket from the bed to wrap around her shivering body and ran out onto the landing and down the stairs. The black Bakelite telephone was practically dancing on top of the hall table, shrilling out its demand for attention. She picked up the handset and stated the area code and two-digit telephone number.

"Sir!" she gasped in response to the caller.

"Yes, sir."

"No, sir."

"Sir."

There was a long pause before she placed the handset back on its base. She turned to find her two roommates, almost buried inside their own blankets, standing on the landing looking down at her.

"What was that about?" Elaine, her black hair practically standing on end, said.

"We heard a great deal of Sir-ing but nothing else," Eugenie said. "Was that Reggie?"

"It was indeed our boss Rear Admiral Reginald Andrews." Krista wrapped the blanket more tightly around her body and started up the stairs. "We are to report for duty wearing our warmest uniform slacks." She reached the landing and stood in front of her friends, waiting for them to move out of her way.

"That was a great many 'Sirs' for such a simple message." Eugenie turned towards the door, almost tripping over the trailing ends of her blanket.

"I was informed that our leader Reggie is to welcome his sister Wren Superintendent Violet Andrews aboard ship today. They are to discuss the outfitting of the ship placed under his command. We are to be ready and available to offer any and all assistance."

"Let me see if I understand the navy-speak correctly." Elaine followed on Eugenie's heels. "Reggie is meeting with his sister Violet and will discuss his needs for the house newly assigned to him with her. We are to stand by in case we are needed. Have I got that right?"

"That is what I understood." Krista walked towards her own room at the front of the cottage.

"Do we have time for breakfast?" Eugenie asked.

"We are to report for duty at ten thirty so we have plenty of time to eat." Krista was thankful that they had, before leaving the cottage. The army might be said to march on its stomach, but the navy sometimes appeared to forget that the Wrens needed to eat and drink.

"So, Wren Superintendent Andrews will be in charge of requisitioning the supplies and equipment!" Eugenie called from her room. "It will be her responsibility to set up whatever Reggie means to make of that house, or I should say 'ship', that has been put under his command." She threw her blanket back on her bed, shivering in the cold air. "Really, the navy's insistence on using naval-speak is quite distracting. I have great difficulty calling a great big house a ship! But needs must, I suppose."

"I still find myself struggling to call a room a 'cabin' and don't get me started on calling buildings 'ships'!" Krista called. "However, I am desperately grateful that Violet is taking care of Reggie's needs and requirements. I dreaded the thought of being responsible for setting up the area set aside for Reggie and whatever his plans are for his people. He has not been exactly clear in what his wants and needs are, has he?"

"You would have a better stab at setting up an office than I ever would!" Eugenie shivered at the thought of removing her warm flannel pyjamas. She didn't enjoy dressing in the cold bedroom space but needs must.

"I was shocked when I saw that open space and all of those desks yesterday!" Elaine called out from her room. "Whatever can the man have planned?"

"It will be up to his sister, our esteemed leader Wren Superintendent Violet Andrews, to rattle information out of him – thankfully." Krista was making her bed.

"Rather her than me." Elaine put the final touch to her bed. "Are we to wear our navy jumpers?"

"That building we were shown around yesterday was freezing." Eugenie hissed when the cold air touched her flesh. "I'm going to wear every piece of warm clothing we have been issued. I doubt very much we will be sitting by the fire today."

"I am wearing a pair of our uniform issue long navy knickers under my slacks," Krista said. "I don't care how they look!"

"Krista, you're not – are you?" Elaine laughed.

"I am going to follow your example." Eugenie turned to her chest of drawers to pull out a pair of the long-legged heavy navy knickers that had been issued to the females serving in the forces. The knickers were the subject of a great deal of mirth – "passion-killers" the women had named them.

When all three were dressed in navy slacks, white woollen shirts and navy jumpers with leather patches at the elbow, leather trim at V-neck and wrists – to prevent fraying – they examined each other to ensure each was shipshape. Then as one they went down the stairs and into the kitchen.

"I want a pot of coffee." Krista had perhaps enough ground beans to make one or two more pots of coffee before she ran out of supplies. Heaven alone knew when she would be able to purchase more coffee grounds. The merchant seamen had been under attack since war was declared in September and supplies of imported items were becoming restricted. Their wonderful landlady, the redoubtable Mrs Marie Fagin, grumbled often about the lack of certain items but she, like every homemaker in Britain, was becoming accustomed to queuing for items that had been readily available in the past.

"I'll put the kettle on the gas stove," Elaine said. "I can't start the day without a pot of tea."

"I'll see what Mrs Fagin has left in the pantry for us," Eugenie said.

"I'm going to light the fire in the range." Krista wasted no time putting on the black coal-residue-encrusted gloves Mrs Fagin kept shoved in the space between the kitchen wall and the range. She opened the range door and using a stick of wood – all metal tools had been donated for the war effort – raked out the ashes in the range fire-pit. She shovelled the ash into an old biscuit box kept for that purpose and put it to one side. "It will warm us before we leave, and the kitchen will be toasty warm for Mrs Fagin when she comes."

"What would we do without Mrs Fagin and her family?" Elaine watched the kettle, almost willing the water to boil.

"We are blessed to have the Fagin family taking care of us." Eugenie backed out of the pantry with eggs, milk, and bread in hand. "Imagine if we had to stand in line waiting for supplies, ordering coal, and keeping the house clean and tidy! It would be a nightmare."

"We would fall into bad health." Krista blew on the knotted paper in the fire grate. "With the unusual hours we are on the go, keeping a home running too would be impossible."

"Great Scott, however did you merit a ship of this size?" Violet Andrews stood in the open area in front of a house sitting inside the medieval curtain walls of Dover Castle. The shouts and noise of men at work carried through the open front door. "Just how many of my Wrens do you imagine seconding to run this ship?"

As a Wren in the Great War and one of the women who fought tooth and nail to re-establish the Wrens for the upcoming conflict, Violet was in her element. She and her brother the rear admiral had been served a delicious breakfast in the officer's mess before walking through the castle and over the ground sheltered inside the wall that surrounded the castle.

"Gloating is an unattractive trait." Reggie, in full naval uniform, stood shoulder to shoulder with his sister for a moment, staring at the house. "I asked Strange to organise this area and, before I could take a breath, she suggested putting you in command. I can captain a ship on the open sea in heavy storms, keep my ship sailing while under fire, but what ... what on earth do I know about clerical chores?" He walked over to the open door and stared in at the sailors frantically laying wires and whatnot. He turned to look at his sister standing proudly in her Wrens uniform.

"No more than I do," she said.

"Then what are you doing here if you cannot help me in my hour of need?" Reggie had been an officer too long and would never show his discomfort by pulling at his collar – but he wanted to.

"You have to be able to articulate your needs." Violet was heartily sick of men mumbling about their wants and needs and expecting women to wave a magic wand and make everything right. "Strangely enough, mind-reading was not gifted to me at birth along with my femininity." Would she be keelhauled if she boxed his ears, she wondered absurdly. "Show me around your ship. Treat me as you would a fellow officer. Discuss your plans with me. I need more information from you than a simple 'set it up'. For heaven's sake, Reggie – use your words!" She was repeating a phrase often used by their childhood nanny.

"Very well." Reggie resisted – barely – sticking his tongue out at his sister. What was it about the woman that almost made him revert to childhood? "Come along. Mind how you step. I would hate to have to listen to you complain about a run in your stockings."

Violet ignored his comment. "Do you have command of the whole ship? Or is this to be a shared space?"

"This is to be my command centre." Reggie led his sister around the three "decks" of his "ship", pointing out features and what he planned for the space.

"You expect males and females to share a room?" She rolled her eyes at his grunt of displeasure at her terminology. "Very well! 'Cabin space'!" Violet stood on the third-floor landing, looking down the staircase. "Very daring of you, Reggie. What about fraternisation? Surely that is to be discouraged?"

"It will be up to your Wrens to keep their virtue intact, woman. There is a war on." Reggie stepped around Violet and led the way back downstairs, through the seamen toiling to get the "ship" ready for launch.

"So many desks." Violet stood in the doorway of the open office space, staring. What on earth was her brother up to?

"Stop dawdling, come along!" Reggie supressed a shudder walking past all the desks. He marched down the length of the first room, through a small windowless room with two desks and into the "cabin" that had been set aside for his use.

He waited until Violet had joined him, closing the door behind her. He removed his hat, throwing it on the desk, one of the few items of furniture in the room, before perching on the front rim of the desk. He simply stared for a moment.

"I am at a loss," he finally said.

"Reggie, what are you up to?" Violet disliked seeing her overbearing brother like this – it was rare for him not to be in command of all around him.

"I have been fighting behind the scenes for years, attempting to set up radio-relay stations." Reggie leaned back on the desk. "I was granted permission to set up in a small way to prove the effectiveness of my idea. Green, Wood and Strange, the three females under my command, have exceeded all my expectations. I had planned to lead from the front." He pushed off the desk to pace.

Violet stood by the window, looking out over the castle grounds towards the curtain wall, and waited.

"It has been a very long time since I was a junior officer," he stopped suddenly to say. "I have been spoiled. I board ship, demand perfection and someone else handles the details."

"Yes, you never have scrubbed the decks," Violet prompted when he seemed lost in thought.

"This war, Violet – we are not ready for it." He continued to pace.

"We are in this war, ready or not, Reggie."

"We are playing catch-up, damn it!" Lord knows they'd had enough warnings but the men in power had closed their ears and eyes to what was clearly to be seen by their underlings. He would not be surprised to learn that Herr Hitler had been planning for this war since before the ink dried on the Treaty of Versailles, the document that ended the Great War, the war that was supposed to end all wars.

"I lived in France for years, Reggie – on the German border, no less." Violet walked across the cabin to take the leather office chair facing the desk. She swung the chair gently from side to side. "In recent years I was horrified by the changes taking place around me." She had lived in Metz, a French town bordering with Germany, teaching English and eking out her funds. It was where she had met Krista for the first time.

"That is neither here nor there." Reggie leaned against the office door. He needed chairs in here asap. "Let me tell you what I plan to achieve."

Violet bit back the "about time" she wanted to say.

CHAPTER 3

Krista, Elaine, and Eugenie rode their motorcycles from the cottage to Dover Castle. The sheepskin-lined leather jackets they wore over their jumpers kept them relatively warm on the short journey. They experienced the expected difficulty entering through security into the castle keep. The men assigned to guard the gates seemed to derive a great deal of amusement from harassing the Wrens.

They didn't leave their motorcycles in the naval garage but rode them directly to the "ship" set aside for Rear Admiral Andrews. If this was going to be their headquarters, they needed to be able to reach it at speed. They ignored the masculine shouts and wolf whistles as they motored along, pulling up in the space outside of their "ship". They parked their bikes and, while pulling off their safety glasses, helmets and gloves, entered the open door.

They walked over wires and through sailors, making their way to the area they had been told would become the main office space.

"We will need somewhere to hang our outside clothing and store our accessories." Krista's voice almost echoed in the large space.

"Make a note of it." Violet Andrews stepped into the room from the opposite end to where the three Wrens stood.

"*Sir!*" The three Wrens came to attention and saluted.

"At ease! For the moment throw your gear over a desktop. There is a latrine along the hallway where you can wash up and brush off the dust from your journey. Report back here as soon as you have restored order to your uniforms. Dismissed!"

Violet turned and marched back to join Reggie.

In his office Reggie waited until Violet had closed the door at her back before saying, "Green, Wood and Strange have travelled the southeast coast of England seeking out emplacement areas for radio masts. They have been bloody marvellous. The work has not been easy but, to give them their due, they never complain. I want teams of young men and women to travel the entire British Isles seeking areas to set up radio towers and relay stations. Some will remain anchored by their towers in order to obtain and relay information about enemy movement, while others will travel between towers. The towers must be manned twenty-four hours a day, seven days a week. We must know what is coming at us – technology has marched ahead in the time since the Great War. I plan to use every advantage of the latest innovative technology."

"Men and women?" Violet raised an eyebrow. She had been disgusted when she overheard one male refer to the women serving in the ATS – the first all-female force to be gathered – as "the soldiers' mattress".

"I have never needed to be responsible for the morals of my men. I expect every man under my leadership to behave as a gentleman while aboard ship," he bit out.

"Reggie, you cannot turn a blind eye to the problems that will arise if you mix male and females and send them out without leadership to keep an eye on them." She was remembering the horrors some of the Wrens in the Great War were subjected to – and by men who were fighting on the same side! You could not deny human nature and consensual fraternisation would occur whatever one did, but no Wren under her command would be subjected to abuse.

She walked to the window again, keeping her back to her brother.

"Your first recruits are all female – why not continue in that vein?" she said.

"I need drivers, radio and Morse Code trained men – and muscle will be needed from time to time I have no doubt." Reggie too had had to discipline men for stepping over the line. It would not be accepted – not under his command. "The only one of my three who can drive is Strange. Have you seen Wood? She is so tiny she would be unable to turn the manual crank on a truck – her feet would never reach a car's pedals never mind a truck's and Lord alone knows how she could see over the steering wheel."

Violet wanted to beat her head off the windowpane. They were getting nowhere. She would have to take charge. At least she was capable of articulating her thoughts. Reggie could counter any suggestion she might make that he did not like.

"Let us see what we have to work with." Violet again opened the door of his inner sanctum and walked through the dark space with two desks and out into the large area lined with desks.

Green, Wood and Strange, their faces shining from the scrubbing they had administered, their uniforms brushed free of all dust, walked into the room. They stood shoulder to shoulder and waited.

Violet gave them a nod. Reggie ignored them for the moment.

"You want this large area turned into an information receiving, gathering and sending station," Violet said. "That is the purpose of all those thick cables being laid through the ship, is it not? You want persons trained to send and receive radio and Morse Code messages – sitting at all these presently empty desks – do I have that right?"

"I thought to have a man on the radio with a Wren capable of taking shorthand to his side. That would speed up the system." The paperwork demanded would be a constant headache. He wished he could pass this headache off to his second-in-command as he could aboard ship – on land, however, he was yet to find a man to serve in that position.

"Two sailors for one job – that is a waste of manpower." Violet turned to stare. "My Wrens can be trained in Morse Code. Some already have been, with great success."

The three Wrens, unsure if they should comment, remained at parade rest.

"Green!" Violet barked.

Elaine straightened and stepped forward.

"You received the highest scores on your Morse code training examination, did you not?"

"Yes, sir." Elaine waited.

"My Wrens took their examination alongside the navy's males," said Violet. "Three outscored all of the sailors taking the exam on the same day. Green came top of the class."

"That is good to know." Reggie wanted to keep these young women close to hand. "I am informed by Strange," he nodded towards Krista who had been raised in France, with French being her mother tongue, "that your spoken French is akin to that of a native, Green." He didn't wait for a response. "I have arranged for you to take driving lessons in the New Year. You will need to pass the driving test quickly – I have need of drivers."

"My mother is an excellent driver," Elaine replied. "If we are to be released over the holiday, I will ask my mother for lessons in the family car." She was so much hoping to receive a pass for the Christmas holiday.

He was not going to comment on the terrifying thought of one woman teaching another to drive. He would have one of his men give her driving lessons and test her proficiency when she returned in the New Year.

"To return to the subject at hand," Violet said, "I will have a list of Wrens trained in Morse code available."

"They will need to be sitting by their receivers day and night," Reggie stated.

"Is that why you want cabins made available to them?" Violet asked.

"Yes." Reggie looked around the room. "Oh, for heaven's sake, Wrens, sit down! You will have to use the desktops but there is no need to stand." He waited until the women were seated. Violet and Krista shared a desktop while Elaine and Eugenie shared a facing desk.

He walked over to the door, opening it slightly and listening. He returned to stand in the aisle in front of the two desks.

"This room," he gestured around, "will be the hub of an information-gathering network. The men and women working in the tunnels will be listening for radio waves and messages from the many ships that sail through the channel. My crew will amass information from the towers that will soon be situated around the country. I will need crew to take messages but equally important I will need despatch riders to carry those messages where they need to go."

"Before we go any further ..." Violet held up a hand. "Krista, is there a notebook and pencil available?"

"There should be." Krista slid from the desktop. While examining the rooms previously she had seen something in the desk drawer of one of the two desks in what she thought of as the dark room – since it had no windows – directly outside the Rear Admiral's office. She hurried to the room, pulling open desk drawers until she found the notebook and pencil she was looking for. She returned to the others.

"Good woman." Violet patted the desktop. "Take notes. Be sure to note we need lockers along one wall of this room."

"Yes, sir." Krista opened the first page of the secretarial notebook and with pencil in hand began to take notes in shorthand.

"We need tea-making equipment too." Reggie wanted a mug of tea right now but had no idea where he might find some. He'd check with the sailors outside. There was no way they were working without some way of making a cuppa. "Green!" he barked. "Request tea from the sailors outside."

"With all due respect, sir, if I ask I will be ignored at best or verbally abused at worse." Elaine didn't move. They had tried to tell Reggie how difficult the sailors made life for them, but he didn't seem to understand. Maybe now he would begin to listen when they tried to tell him of the sailors' attitude towards the Wrens.

"Allow me, sir." Eugenie hopped down from the desktop.

Reggie looked like he was about to explode.

"I know where the galley is." Really, men! This was a house for all they called it a ship and even aboard ships there was usually a galley. There was a kitchen in this house, for heaven's sake! She had seen it on the tour they had been given yesterday. "A pot of tea coming up!"

She didn't wait for permission but left the room, turning in the direction of the rear of the house. She crossed her fingers, hoping that the area had been left untouched.

"*Perkins, follow that female!*" a chief petty officer barked.

Eugenie heard him mutter under his breath that there was no place for females aboard ship.

"*Sir!*" A sailor dropped the thick cables he was holding to the deck and followed smartly on the female's heels.

While Eugenie was heading for the galley, Reggie began to pace while spitting out ideas. Krista kept note of everything he mentioned while he skipped from one idea to another.

Violet listened to her brother state his plans – horrified yet fascinated. The task before them was mammoth. Reggie pointed to walls that would shield transmitters, transformers, batteries and more. His information-gathering hub was to be staffed twenty-four hours a day seven days a week.

"Reggie, one man cannot run this operation. You need a command force. You cannot be everywhere and do everything. You need to delegate."

Krista, still frantically taking notes, raised her eyes from her notepad and stared at Elaine. What did all of this have to do with them?

"I agree with you, Violet." Reggie waved his arms about. "But this, this will be the nerve centre. The information from the teams we will send out must come through here. Someone must know what is going on around the country land, sea, and air."

Violet stared at her brother in awe. The man was a genius. It was a daunting task but she would do everything in her power to help him.

"The teams you plan to send out . . ." Violet held onto the desk rim, leaning back and looking at the ceiling. "They will need to receive specialist training. A place must be chosen for that training. We need a basic structure in place before we gather your teams."

"Green, Wood and Strange received no specialist training," Reggie objected. "They got out there and got the job done. That is the kind of crew I am looking for."

"If I might make a suggestion?" Krista was glad to rest her wrist.

"Speak freely." Reggie would take all the help he could get.

"The army has many training bases scattered around the country." Krista had been trained on one such base before travelling to Germany with her friend Peregrine Fotheringham-Carter. "Captain Waters has something similar to your idea for the crews you wish to send out in place already."

"You see!" Reggie declared. "This is what I am talking about. The right hand doesn't know what the left hand is doing. Churchill has been demanding it for months and I agree with him. We must have open communication between the services. It is imperative. Good show, Strange."

A sharp knock on the door sounded.

"*Enter!*" Reggie shouted.

A smiling Eugenie. followed by a blushing Perkins holding a heavy tray, entered the room.

"Tea, sir?" Eugenie gestured to a desktop, directing Perkins to put the tray down.

"Not before time!" Reggie barked. "Dismissed, sailor!"

CHAPTER 4

"Ladies," Reggie perched on a desktop, a thick white mug of tea in hand, "there is a great deal to be done to prepare the ship that has been placed under my command. Hitler's forces are showing us up in the South Atlantic at this very moment. They were prepared for the off – we need to play catch-up. We have the winter to prepare."

"The navy is making noises about removing you three from Rear Admiral Andrew's command," said Violet. "You cannot assist in the setting up of this ship – you would only be in the way and at loose ends. With that in mind I have arranged special training for you." She ignored the barely muffled groans from the three young women. "You will report to the Wrennery at 0700 tomorrow. You will receive further orders then. Do the Wrens proud, ladies!"

"You are all three to be released from my direct command until the New Year. Green, Wood and Strange, you three women have performed the duties asked of you marvellously." Reggie was finding it difficult to meet their eyes. "Green, Wood, I will have passes covering the holidays issued for each of you. When you return to Dover in the New Year you can no longer remain as a group."

"We can go home for Christmas!" Elaine gasped, ignoring all other matters.

"Do you know where we will be sent in the New Year?" Eugenie prayed the forces would not return her to office work.

Krista remained silent.

"In the New Year you will again be under my command." Reggie would make certain of that. "Until then you will attend the special classes set up for your group. I will have your passes issued. That does not mean that you will be lolling about over the holiday period. Wood . . ." He waited until he was sure he had the young woman's attention before continuing. "You were a three-day eventer, were you not?" He had read her files.

"Yes, sir." Eugenie didn't add that she had been a much-decorated member of that cadre of riders who risked their necks on the backs of some of the nation's most difficult to handle horses and indeed courses.

"Do you know of any of your fellow riders who have joined the Wrens?" Reggie did not have time to wait while his sister searched through the thousands of applications from young women to find what he sought.

"I'm not sure, sir," Eugenie replied. "I would have more of an idea when I return home. The gossip in the stables would keep me up to date. May I ask why you need three-day eventers?"

"I will need despatch riders."

"Most if not all of my friends have sent their horses away for the duration of the war, sir." Eugenie too had sent her main horses away from the danger to come. She did not wish to have her horses requisitioned for war as they had been in the Great War. She had sent her horses to Ireland but a great many of her fellow riders had chosen to send theirs to America and Canada.

"I had not intended to send out horse riders!" Reggie almost laughed at the idea. "We could not afford to keep horses anyway. No, I need some of those 'neck or nothing' riders to learn to ride motorcycles." Those who rode their mounts 'neck or nothing' were the most daring of riders, taking risks with their mounts and their own necks that he personally considered insane. But he would need riders who were not afraid to continue carrying messages when bombs started to fall – and bombs would fall – Hitler would never obey the rules of war and protect innocent civilians.

"Reggie, that is brilliant." Violet knew they had daring women apply for the Wrens. She would have the secretaries begin to search for athletes – women who took part in dangerous outdoor sports would be ideal for the special crews her brother needed. Yes indeed, her Wrens would shine.

Krista and Elaine listened, fascinated. It was a world neither knew anything of.

"I will make enquiries when I return home, sir." Eugenie knew just who to ask too. "Would they have to join the Wrens?"

"It would be better if they were already Wrens." Reggie thought it was asking a great deal but needs must. "If they had already been through training, they could take up their duties immediately with you as leader. They must be willing to jump to your every command." He looked at the almost fairy-like young woman sitting on the desk – her feet didn't even touch the floor. He wondered if he was asking the impossible.

"I am well respected within the three-day eventer community, sir." Eugenie knew her reputation with other riders would serve her well. "Being in command of the despatch riders you seek will not be a problem. But if I might make a suggestion?"

"Speak freely!" Reggie waved a hand.

"It might suit your needs better to seek out the female grooms that handle the horses and the work it entails daily." She knew a great many of her fellow riders had travelled overseas with their horses. They had not taken any but their favourite grooms with them. "Those young women are accustomed to following orders, working in less than ideal conditions, and many – because of the world travel involved – while not being fluent, can make themselves understood in a second if not a third language."

"I had given no thought to grooms." Reggie almost groaned. What did he know of horses and the young women who took care of them? "Your mission, Wood, is to find – a dozen would be ideal but six will do at a pinch – I need young women who are ambitious and daring. I will leave that in your hands."

"Yes, sir," Eugenie found the demand daunting but exciting too. She might not be riding a mountain of four-legged muscle but there were many tricks she had employed on her motorcycle. She would share her knowledge with her team.

Krista and Elaine listened and wondered what the future held for them. Yes, they had trained with the Wrens but, because each had a parent not born in the United Kingdom, they could not actually join any of the armed forces.

"Will I be returning to Dover Castle and the cottage in the New Year, sir?" Elaine dared to ask.

"We shall see," was all Reggie was willing to say. Who knew what might happen from one day to the next?

"Strange . . ."

"Sir." Krista was almost sick with nerves.

"Clarence Brownlow-Hastings has requested –" Reggie began.

"No," Krista stated emphatically.

Elaine almost fell off the desk. Had Krista just said *no*? Were they allowed to pick and choose what they would and would not do?

"*Strange!*" Reggie barked.

"Respectfully, sir, I will not be under that man's control under any circumstances." The very thought made her ill. The man had thought to turn her whore for his benefit. She would rather shoot him between those raptor eyes of his.

"*Strange, would you allow me to speak!*" Reggie practically shouted.

"Sorry, sir, just the mention of that man's name puts my teeth on edge."

She opened her mouth to add more but Reggie's upheld stiffened finger stopped her.

Elaine and Eugenie exchanged glances. Fascinated but not understanding what was going on, they remained silent and settled in to listen.

Violet understood completely and agreed with Krista. There was no way she would allow the young woman she considered her ward to be placed under that man's control.

"Strange, as I started to say before I was interrupted ..." He waited to see if he could continue, absentmindedly wondering when was the last time he'd been treated in such a manner. It had been many years ago.

"There are a great many people in the forces who wish to have you under their direct command." Reggie had been fighting to keep this young woman with him. He was not about to relinquish her now when his need was at its greatest. "I have requested that you be assigned to me but, as with many things, the paperwork has not come through yet." He pinched his nose and sighed. "I have been granted permission to retain Wood and Green but you, miss ..." he glared, "are causing me a great deal of difficulty. I need you to keep a civil tongue in your head and, if questioned before I have the necessary paperwork in hand, claim ignorance."

"That should not be too difficult." Krista sighed. "I have not understood anything you have said." She turned to her two friends. "Have you two?"

"Smile prettily, bite your tongue and pretend stupidity if anyone tries to order you about," Eugenie said. "Have I got that right, sir?"

"That about sums it up," Reggie was forced to agree.

Krista thought her wrist would break as she struggled to keep recording the question-and-answer session that evolved while the four women questioned Reggie closely on his wants and needs. She silently prayed she was not expected to type up all of her notes. Surely one of the Wrens in the typing pool could take care of that chore?

It was three weary Wrens who drove their motorcycles through the dark Dover streets heading for the cottage they called home. Each of them silently blessed Mrs Fagin when they entered the warm rooms and smelled the delicious aroma of whatever she had left on the back of the range for them to eat. They were so hungry they didn't care what mystery ingredients today's stew might hold.

"I am frozen!" Krista hung her jacket on a hook behind the entrance door. She put her helmet, safety goggles and gloves on the hall table. She would take them upstairs when she went.

"Well, Strange," Elaine asked, "did your navy passion-killer knickers make a difference?"

"They kept my nether region comfortably warm – thank you very much." Krista laughed.

"Mine practically go down to my feet." Eugenie giggled as she too removed her outer wear. "I have to admit I was glad of the additional warmth on the ride home."

The three friends walked into the kitchen and, after washing their hands at the kitchen sink, began to set up for their meal. Krista pulled the stew to the front of the range, Eugenie set the table while Elaine fetched items from the pantry.

They hurriedly prepared the meal and sat down to eat.

"Can you believe we are going to be allowed home for Christmas?" Elaine's voice broke through the silence that had fallen as each woman enjoyed the thick stew that Mrs Fagin had prepared for them.

"If one listens to the whispers about this war, it may well be the last Christmas we enjoy in relative peace," Eugenie looked up from her almost empty bowl to say.

"You would have far more of an idea of the navy's position on holidays, Elaine. Your father is a captain in the navy. I doubt he arrived home every Christmas." Krista was thinking of the letter she had received from Lia Caulfield, the woman who had employed her upon her arrival in England. Lia was the wife of a naval captain and had become a friend. She had enclosed notes from the twins David and Edward with her letter. How she missed those little mischief-makers. Lia and the twins would be spending Christmas in Norfolk with her husband's family.

"That is true," Elaine nodded, her dark hair dancing around her face, "but my father was often on the open seas. We are sitting in an English cottage, for goodness' sake! We can travel to our homes for the holiday."

"Won't it be marvellous!" Eugenie clapped her hands in glee.

Krista sat and listened to them chatter like excited children as they tried to imagine the pleasure of a home visit over the holiday. Elaine and Eugenie almost danced on their chair seats as they each made plans to reach their homes in the quickest, most efficient way possible.

"I'll put the kettle on," Krista said when there appeared to be no end to the delights each of her companions were imagining. She didn't wait for a response but carried her empty bowl and cutlery to the sink. She pulled the heavy black kettle from the back of the range. They had learned to keep a kettle filled with water at the back of the range, ready to pull it forward over the fire and prepare a pot of the tea. The additional hot water would be used to wash the dishes.

She listened to her friends as they continued to discuss and plan their holiday adventures. She was not envious of them. She simply didn't understand the concept of a family holiday. She grew up in the Auberge du

Ville, a hotel, where holidays simply meant more work and longer hours. She had spent last Christmas alone in the Caulfield house in London and had enjoyed the chance to simply cater to her own wants and needs.

She hoped that she could remain in the cottage over the holiday period. She had nowhere else to go.

CHAPTER 5

"Would anyone care to make a guess about our special training?" Elaine held her hands out to the flames of the gas stove.

All three women were dressed in their navy uniform slacks, shirts and jumpers. They were standing grouped around the gas stove, holding their hands out to the flames, trying to get warm. The December morning was freezing and since they had to leave soon there was no point in lighting a fire.

"I really don't care." Eugenie shivered. "I just hope that whatever we're doing it's somewhere warm."

Krista went to stir the pot of porridge on the stovetop. "Why am I doing this again?" she said, staring at the unappetising gruel in disgust.

"Because, according to my nanny," Eugenie smirked, "it will warm the cockles of your heart – and no – before you ask, Krista – I have no idea what that means. Besides, I'm very proud of myself for remembering to put the oatmeal to soak overnight."

"My grandmother always said a good bowl of porridge first thing in the morning will stick to your ribs!" Elaine said.

"Well, sticky ribs or warm cockles, it is ready." Krista raised the spoon from the pot to inspect the consistency. "The tea and coffee need to be poured and ..." with a glance at the kitchen clock, "we need to get going soon."

"Strange, Green, Wood, I presume?"

The women had arrived at the large Wrennery building, parked their motorcycles outside the door and now, with their leather jackets, helmets, gloves, and goggles under their arms, stood in the vestibule of the building.

"I am Leading Wren Baxter. I have your orders." The tall stern-faced woman was unknown to the trio. With a clipboard clutched tightly to her chest, she practically marched across the marble vestibule floor in their direction.

"*Green!*" she barked.

"Ma'am!" Elaine came to attention. She was never sure of the proper term of address. Should it be sir or ma'am? Well, if she was wrong the woman would correct her.

"You will park your motorcycle in one of the outbuildings before returning here to take the ferry to the motor pool. Seaman Archer is standing by to instruct you on motor-engine care." She tore a piece of paper loose from the clipboard and passed it to Green.

"*Wood!*"

"Yes, ma'am!" Eugenie struggled to come to attention and hold onto her outer wear.

"You are to be on loan to the ATS." She looked over her clipboard to stare down at Wood. "You will be instructing ATS officers on the care and handling of horses." She had begun to tear another piece of paper loose when she stopped for a moment. "We are hoping you can help the officers understand the handling of horses. This is vital as we will not have enough petrol for mechanical farm equipment. The women you will be instructing are city gals for the most part. They have only ever seen horses pulling carts in the street. Any help that you can give to them will be appreciated, I'm sure." She tore the paper off and passed it to Wood.

"*Strange!*"

"Thank you, Baxter." Andorra Prendergast strode across the floor, her impressive figure commanding the decks. "I will take it from here."

"Ma'am," Baxter turned on her heel and quick-marched back to wherever in the large ship she had come from.

"Wrens, with me!" Andorra turned and, without waiting to see if they followed, marched back into the depths of the Wrennery.

The four women marched without speaking to the rear of the ship. Andorra opened a door and a welcome glow of electric light and warmth escaped into the corridor. She waited for the other three women to step inside a square room with no windows and a selection of mismatched soft armchairs. The glowing fire was a welcome sight to the three who had ridden their motorcycles through the freezing winter wind.

"This must have been the housekeeper or cook's quarters, don't you think?" Andorra pulled her hat from her head while closing the door. "We have changed its use." She threw her hat onto one of the mismatched soft armchairs that were pulled around the brightly burning fire. "Which is neither here nor there." She threw her elegant body into one of the chairs. "Take a seat, ladies!" She sighed deeply while examining the three women. "Wrens, I am ready to mutiny, and I never thought those words would ever pass my lips." She closed her eyes and leaned into the back of the chair.

"Do stop being so dramatic, Andorra!" Eugenie threw her outdoor clothing onto one of the spare armchairs before sitting down. Krista and Elaine did the same.

"I am so frustrated by the way we Wrens are being treated. I want to scream and physically attack something or someone." Andorra sat upright. "This is one of the few places that we Wrens can cut loose."

The women jerked slightly when a sharp knock sounded on the wood of the door. Without waiting for permission, a smiling young woman in white stuck her head around the partially open door.

"A pot of tea for four, Captain?"

"Bless you, Cox, yes," Andorra replied, not at all disturbed by the lack of formality. "And something to nibble on if at all possible. We can put the teapot on the hearth to keep warm."

The door closed.

"Gertrude Cox is, or I suppose was, a member of my crew." Andorra was a highly decorated internationally renowned yachtswoman. "She has been reduced to a glorified waitress by the powers that be."

"Andorra, what are we doing here?" Eugenie wondered aloud.

"We are fighting a war."

"We are aware of that," Eugenie said dryly.

"No, the war I speak of is within what should be our own ranks." Andorra crossed her legs and stared at the three women. "The Wrens are being set up for failure at every turn." She jumped to her feet when a thud sounded on the door. She crossed the room swiftly to open it.

Cox struggled into the room with a large well-loaded tray.

"Sorry about kicking the door. My hands are full as you can see." Cox looked around the room for somewhere to set the tray. "The galley of this ship is the next cabin along. There is always a tea urn on the go."

Krista had already made a quick examination of the room and noticed several folding tables stacked against the wall. She stood and began unfolding one of the tables, checking it was secure before gesturing to Cox who set the tray on its surface.

"If you need anything else, Captain – give me a shout." Without waiting for a reply, Cox quickly left the cabin, closing the door sharply.

"The women presently in the Wrens, indeed in all of the forces, are being sabotaged from within their own ranks." Andorra continued the conversation she had started before being interrupted. She walked over to the table and began pouring milk from the tall jug on the tray into four thick white enamel mugs. She lifted the heavy teapot, using the handle and the extra handle over the spout of the teapot which eased the weight of the heavy pot. "Help yourselves to sugar and a biscuit." She carried the teapot to the hearth. The flames from the fire would keep the tea hot.

When they were again seated, mugs of tea to hand, she said, "We are fighting a war, ladies, make no mistake. Female against males and it is only going to get worse as more women are called up to serve."

The women drank their tea, glad of the heat it offered after the cold of the morning.

"I believe there has been talk of a pass over the holidays for you three," Andorra said. "I won't interfere with this, I assure you. I don't know how much assistance you can offer me – but I am desperate. Wood ..."

Eugenie sipped her tea and waited.

"You are ordered to assist a group of women from the ATS to become familiar with the care of horses." Andorra shook her head sadly. "The women you are being asked to help are eager to learn but they have never been around livestock in their lives. I would have thought this misplacement of personnel a clerical error if the same sort of thing wasn't happening all over the ship. There are women within the ATS who have backgrounds in farming and others who had their own horses. These women are not being asked to lead." She gulped her tea, trying desperately not to curse the men in charge. "There is a very strong betting pool within the ranks as to who can make the most women cry. There is an extra pot of money for those who actually cause females to pack their bags and return to the kitchen!"

"Surely this has not come as a surprise to you, Andorra." Elaine stood and began to take the mugs from the others for a refill. The first mug of tea had quickly disappeared. "The treatment we received during our training in Portsmouth must have given you a heads-up as to the attitude of the men."

Krista watched Elaine throw the slop into a bowl before adding milk to the mugs.

"We are going to war!" Andorra was trying not to shout. "We will be up against the forces of a madman. *This is not the time for fighting within the ranks!*" She fought to get herself under control. "The saddest thing in all of this – to my eyes anyway, ladies – is that the rot appears to be starting from the top."

"What do you want of us?" Eugenie was quite sure that Andorra had a plan.

Andorra accepted a mug from Elaine. "I know all three of you. I trained with you. I know the orders you received this morning." She paused to sip at her tea. "What I am asking of all three of you is to turn into tattletales. I know it goes against the grain, but I must have information if I am to improve the lot of women in this blessed war."

"You are taking rather a lot on your own shoulders." Elaine finished serving and sat with her own mug in hand.

"I am not alone in my efforts," Andorra said. "I was drafted to speak with you three because we know each other. The women joining the forces must learn to work within the chain of command and this is proving to be a problem. There are women crying to officers not within their own chain of command, which is as you know a strict no-no. It simply is not done but, since most women have never been part of a crew, they have no understanding of how matters stand."

"My father, the naval captain," Elaine smiled, "has spoken with me at length about this problem. Father states that women have traditionally worked alone – they have no knowledge of the unwritten rules of teamwork."

"I beg to differ!" Eugenie snapped.

"I cannot comment." Krista had no idea what they were talking about – not for the first time.

"Think about it, ladies." Andorra leaned forward to stare. "We women have long been accustomed to entertaining ourselves. Some have crafts to occupy their hands if not their minds – others read – even horse-riding is a solitary pursuit. There are very few of us women who have played team sports. Men, it appears, learn to understand the rules of the game from the time they start playing team sports. We are at a disadvantage from the get-go but we must learn and learn quickly."

"What can we do?" Krista asked.

"Spy for me," Andorra said. "I need to know what is happening in the ranks. You three are being sent in different directions. Wood, you will observe the treatment of the ATS females and report back to me. Green, the attitude of the men in the motor pool is causing a great deal of problems. Strange, you will be observing the training of our own Wrens." She captured the eyes of each of them. "I need you to report directly to me. I will guide you through the actions you may need to take to tackle any problems that arise. I have years of training in command structure. I will share that knowledge with all of you."

"You are setting us an almost impossible task," Eugenie said.

"I am aware of that," Andorra agreed. "But it is imperative that we set our standards now before we are swept up willy-nilly into war. We have at the most three months to try and set our ranks in order."

"I have no idea of my orders," Krista said, "but I have no objection to keeping you informed."

"I too will keep you informed," Elaine said.

"Who am I to rock the boat?" Eugenie shrugged.

"Thank you, ladies." Andorra sighed. "I am so glad that you have a telephone at that cottage of yours."

"That line is not secure." Krista didn't think it would be a good idea to discuss problems within the ranks over an open telephone line.

"I am aware." Andorra nodded. "There is nothing to stop me telephoning to share gossip. Then of course you must invite me over to share a pot of tea or if we can get Krista to share her supply of coffee. Why, we can have the most delightful time together, can we not?"

CHAPTER 6

Krista sat on a narrow bench seat in the back of a canvas-covered lorry. She was tightly squeezed into the space, surrounded by excited Wrens. She had been ordered into this ferry, as the navy insisted on calling any vehicle that carried personnel from post to post. She'd been introduced to the other Wrens – there were too many names for her to try to remember. She dug her boots into the bed of the truck, trying to keep her balance as the driver seemed to find every problem spot in the road. As female screams and struggles to remain seated echoed around her, the sound of male laughter carried from the driver's section of the lorry.

She gritted her teeth, determined to endure. They travelled along roads they could not see, waiting to discover whatever awaited them at the end of the journey. The lorry came to a jarring stop without any warning being given, throwing the women around.

"Okay, you lot!" A hard slap at the canvas cover sounded. "Jump out and let's be seeing yeh!"

"Ladies!" Krista stood and picked her way through the tumbled bodies to the back opening.

"*Look out, boys!*" someone shouted from outside the lorry. "*Here comes the ball-buster!*"

"Strange!" Andorra, dressed similarly to Krista in slacks and leather jacket, appeared at the rear of the lorry. "I brought your motorcycle." She didn't wait for comment. "Let me give you a hand helping the others down."

Krista jumped down and, between them, she and Andorra unlocked and lowered the tailgate.

Under the jeering and abusive comments of a group of seamen standing smoking and enjoying the show, Krista and Andorra gave a hand and instructions on the correct way to exit the lorry. The sight of stocking tops and bare thighs greatly added to the seamen's enjoyment.

When the women were safely out of the lorry, Krista turned to look around her. The scene was a familiar one to her. She had been somewhere similar in the past. They were out in the country – fields of green stretched as far as the eye could see. There were Nissen huts dotted around the fields with men marching and shouting close to where they stood.

"*Wrens, form ranks!*" Andorra shouted.

She tried not to grimace at the pathetic attempt by the women to arrange their uniforms and form up in ranks as they had been taught. The sneering, jeering comments being shouted at them by the seamen didn't help.

When they were finally in a semblance of formation she shouted. "*Quick march!*"

She set off across the fields, thankful the cold had frozen the earth and they were not forced to march through watery muck. She kept her eyes focused on the pre-fabricated Nissen building that had been put to their use for training purposes.

One of the doors of the Nissan hut was opened from the inside.

"*Wrens, single file!*" Andorra stopped to one side of the open door. "*Strange, with me!*"

"*Sir!*" Krista marched smartly and saluted before taking her place at Andorra's side.

"Look here, lads! There's more of them women wanting to be men. Like wearing the trousers, do you then, sweetheart?"

That and other far more impolite comments were shouted in Andorra and Krista's direction, but they ignored all of them while they watched the women step into the Nissan hut.

The door was closed at their backs.

"Strange, with me!" Andorra snapped and marched a few steps towards a second door opening into the Nissan hut. She opened the door and stepped inside. She waited until Krista was inside before closing the door. "We are using the second room, which is much larger, as a classroom. This," she gestured around, "is supposed to be an office."

The room they stood in was cold with a large window, a desk and telephone but not much else.

Krista shoved her hands into her sheepskin-lined leather jacket, glad of its warmth. The room was freezing. She hoped the main room the Wrens were using as a classroom had some form of heat. She walked over to a large window that faced open fields.

"Andorra," she looked over her shoulder to say, "the journey to this base was a disgrace. The driver appeared to seek out every pothole in the road. He delighted in every scream and wail that came from the Wrens who were shaken violently about the ferry. We have been subjected to this kind of behaviour from the moment we put ourselves forward for training." She paused. "Tell me – surely you faced something similar when you decided to compete against men in yacht-racing?"

"One always hopes that matters will change for the better." Andorra joined Krista at the window. She leaned her shoulder against the cold Plexiglas. "Why can these men," she nodded towards the seamen working around the fields, "not see that they need us and not as bloody maids and cleaners?"

"May I politely suggest that you are fighting the wrong war, Andorra. You cannot focus on changing men's attitudes. What you need to concentrate on – if I might be allowed to say – is making your Wrens the best they can be. It is not fair, but women have to be better and work harder than the men. We cannot fight Hitler and the battle of the sexes. Focus on what you can achieve and leave the impossible for another time and place."

"You are not the first to tell me that." Andorra wanted to bang her head off the wall.

"In my opinion," Krista said, "what needs to be done is to acknowledge the problems without dwelling on them. The women need to be toughened up. That lorry drive was a nightmare and a disgrace." She waited to see if Andorra had anything to say before continuing. "The driver of the vehicle behaved in a reprehensible fashion. But, Andorra," she turned to stare at the other woman, "the women were not helping themselves. They were all wearing skirts, for goodness' sake! That is the fault of their officers. They should have been ordered to wear their uniform slacks as they were coming to mucky fields not paved roads. The slacks would have made exiting the ferry a great deal more dignified and denied the leering men some of their pleasure."

"But the men seem to object most forcefully to women wearing slacks," Andorra said.

"They are going to moan anyway – most vocally. Let them." Krista had been embarrassed for the women in the lorry with her. They had not behaved as she expected trained Wrens to behave with their shrieking and crying.

"We are being set up to fail!" Andorra snapped. "Look at this!" She waved towards the view out the window. "Bloody fields as far as the eye can see. I am a sailor. I command the sea. Not daisies and buttercups."

"You're being too impatient!"

"Not the first time I've heard that." Andorra smiled.

"What is this place anyway?"

"Training grounds for the rank and file. They have to have somewhere to learn to march in step." She stepped away from the window, walked across the room and perched on the rim of the desk. "But this is not what I brought you here for."

"You mean, there is more?" Krista felt her heart sink. She was not even a real Wren. What was she doing here?

"Have a seat." Andorra patted the desktop. "This thing is sturdy and should bear our weight." She didn't speak at first when Krista joined her on the desktop, merely staring intently before saying in a whisper, "Krista, I've spoken with Captain Waters. I know of your experience in Europe and the training you received before you made that journey." She waited to see how Krista would respond.

"Indeed." Krista felt her spine stiffening. The mission she had carried out in Europe had been secret. What was she allowed to say?

"I have been assured by all I approached that you are the soul of discretion. I need advice, Krista – in truth. I am becoming desperate."

"Andorra, why don't you tell me what it is you need from me?"

"I have been charged with assembling a female group of espionage agents."

Andorra's voice was so low Krista was having difficulty hearing her and leaned in closer.

"The women must be able sailors first and foremost. They will be trained, as you were, to crawl through muck silently and scale obstacles. The same as the men. They will be taught to shoot and assemble explosives." She closed her eyes briefly before snapping them open to stare at Krista. "You have just seen a selection of the women who have joined our ranks. How can I ask any of those wailing flibbertigibbets to undertake such a mission?"

"You are being unfair, Andorra. The Wrens in that ferry this morning – from listening to them speak – they have all come directly from all-girl boarding schools. They have been sheltered and protected from men and indeed the world all of their lives. You cannot expect them to be ready to jump into danger like some form of super-spy."

"But if I choose my crew badly the women under my command will die!" Andorra wailed in a whisper.

"Andorra, we are at war. We could all of us die at any minute. Nowhere will be safe."

"Let's get out of here and find some heat." Andorra abruptly got off the desk. "It's bloomin' freezing in here."

The two women left the Nissan hut and Andorra led the way to where she had securely stashed Krista's motorcycle.

"Hop on the back," Andorra said.

"Since this is my motorcycle," Krista stepped forward, "why don't you hop on the back?"

"You don't know where we're going."

"Very true!" Krista laughed, glad of a moment's light-heartedness'. "I suppose I'll take the back seat then." She threw her leg over the rear wheel and waited.

The motorcycle rolled forward through ruts spaced along the fields. The two women leaned forward, desperate now to find somewhere with heat. The journey thankfully wasn't long. Andorra pulled the motorcycle onto the grass verge surrounding a group of small cottages hidden in a slight rise in the landscape.

"We have been given these cottages for our use," Andorra said as soon as she'd turned off the motor. "Each has a rather primitive WC but there is a range, a water pump and, thankfully, plenty of wood to burn. Come inside." She held the motorcycle while Krista dismounted.

The two women walked along the garden path. If there had ever been flowers in the garden they had long been marched underfoot. The place had a bleak feeling to it. They hurried towards the grey painted door of the cottage. They sighed as one at being out of the wind when they stepped inside.

"*Permission to come aboard!*" Andorra shouted, walking briskly down a narrow hall. She didn't wait for a response and, with Krista at her heels, stepped down a granite step into a brightly lit kitchen.

"I hope you were not expecting me to pipe you aboard, Captain!" Gertrude Cox turned from the pot she was stirring on the range top.

"Cox, tell me you have a pot of tea going!" Andorra hurried over to the range. "We are perishing."

"It won't take me a moment to get one going." Cox pulled a kettle from the back of the range.

"Krista, I don't believe I introduced you to Wren Gertrude Cox when she served us tea at the Wrennery?"

The introductions were made while the tea brewed and the two women who had come in from the cold tried to defrost their shivering bodies in the welcome warmth of the kitchen.

"We have four more joining us." Andorra, in spite of being cold, removed her jacket. One simply did not wear one's outdoor clothing indoors. She hung the jacket on one of the nails protruding from the back of the kitchen door. "Krista, we wish to pick your brain."

"Andorra, I cannot believe I have any expertise to offer. I know nothing about sailing. I am not even a real Wren," Krista objected while also removing her jacket and hanging it on a nail.

"You have received training in matters that we know nothing about." Andorra gratefully accepted the mug of tea Cox handed her. She carried the mug over to the large kitchen table standing in the middle of the kitchen floor. She took a seat and held the hot mug between her hands, desperately needing the heat.

"We are, all of us who served under the captain, fit and healthy women who love sailing and being on the open sea." Cox put a jug of milk and a bowl of sugar on the table. She placed a mug in front of Krista before taking a seat with her own mug in hand. "We know nothing of land-grubbing." She wrinkled her nose at the very thought.

"All of my crew can shoot." Andorra held the mug against her forehead. She was still cold. "We shoot flares, we have weapons in case of attack by large sea creatures. We have never shot at another human, although in certain waters there is an element of danger from pirates and one must be prepared."

Cox leaned over the table to stare at Krista. "Strange, we are being tasked with something we feel unqualified to do but we desperately want to help. You've crawled through muck while being shouted at by hairy-handed cretins. That is more than we have done." She gestured between herself and Andorra.

"I thought you were a galley servant." Krista sipped her tea, wondering what she had landed in.

"Oh, Cox goes wherever she feels like going!" Andorra laughed. "I've never seen anyone try to stop her."

Before more could be said the back door opened and women almost tumbled into the warm space.

CHAPTER 7

"Thank the Lord, heat!" Elaine groaned, stepping into the cottage. "I am frozen to the bone!"

"Wood is already upstairs." Krista who had been the first to reach home, was standing in the kitchen doorway. "Hurry up and change. Mrs Fagin has left us what she called a hearty rabbit stew."

"I need to wash." Elaine started to climb the stairs.

"We'll be having guests this evening!" Krista called after her.

"You can fill me in when I come down – after I have a wash!" Elaine hurried up the stairs.

"I am seriously thinking of getting a paraffin heater for my room!" Eugenie shouted from her room to Elaine while they removed their uniforms. "These rooms are freezing!"

"My mother won't have one of those heaters in the house!" Elaine called back. "She says they are dangerous, and they stink! We wouldn't want our clothes and bedding stinking of paraffin!"

"I suppose but I am dreadfully tired of being cold!"

"I am going to have a quick wash down before I change!" Elaine hurried into the bathroom across the hall from the bedrooms. She silently thanked Mrs Fagin for having a gas water heater installed in the bathroom. She needed to feel clean.

Krista and Eugenie were in the kitchen devouring bowls of rich rabbit stew when Elaine finally made it downstairs.

"As I said, we are having guests this evening." Krista eyed Elaine's pyjamas and dressing gown.

"I needed to be comfortable. I'll get dressed after we eat but, honestly, I needed the comfort of something familiar."

"We couldn't wait for you to get down here." Eugenie didn't care what anyone was wearing. "We were weak with hunger. Mrs Fagin has surpassed herself with this stew."

"The pot is on the back of the range." Krista jerked her head towards the range. "We've already set your place at table."

Elaine took the bowl sitting on the table and began to ladle stew into it.

"What happened today?" Eugenie asked.

"I have never been subjected to such a disagreeable day in my life." Elaine sat down and took her first mouthful of the stew. "Bless Mrs Fagin," she muttered.

"What happened?" Krista prompted.

"The men in the motor pool have developed fiendish ways of making any female silly enough to step into their lair miserable." Elaine continued to eat as she spoke. "A particular favourite is to wait until one is under the bonnet of a car and then ..." She stopped a moment. "I can only refer to it as abuse of one's derriere. A large hairy hand is used to viciously slap and pinch one's derriere. Which of course causes the poor female so abused to jerk in shock, bang her head off the underside of the bonnet, collapse the wire holding the bonnet upright and bring it crashing down onto her unfortunate head, mashing her face into the engine. I assure you it causes almost hysterical laughter among the men. That is just one of the many delightful ways one is welcomed into the motor pool."

"One presumes you were abused in just such a fashion?" Eugenie asked.

"I was."

"How did you react?" Krista was curious. Elaine was not someone who would weep and wail.

"I have three brothers as you know. While they have never actually abused my derriere, I have been subjected to their infantile idea of amusement. I knew the worst thing in the world I could do was give them something to snigger over. I raised the engine bonnet very slowly, lowered my legs to the floor and simply stared at the person who had caused my accident. I looked – again very slowly – from his feet to his receding hairline and informed him that the gentlemen of my acquaintance normally wined and dined me before attempting to take advantage. I then informed him of the problem I'd found with the engine and walked away."

"Good for you!" Krista said.

"It was miserable, to be honest," Elaine said. "I couldn't relax. It was almost like walking through an obstacle course. One had to be alert at every moment. It was exhausting."

"How did you know there was a problem with the engine?" Eugenie hadn't known Elaine knew anything about engines.

"I know nothing about driving a car or van, but I discovered to my surprise that an engine is an engine. I know boats and have worked with my brothers on different boat engines since childhood."

"That was fortunate," Eugenie remarked. "So, the men of the motor pool never offered you a driving lesson?"

"I don't believe I would trust any one of the men I met today to give me driving lessons. I would need to arm myself with a blunt object to protect my virtue. Imagine being out on the open road with one of those cretins!"

"My day was vastly different." Eugenie stood to refill her bowl. "I'm afraid I almost ran out of patience with the women under my command and boxed ears. They are willing," she turned from the range to say, "I won't deny that, but do they have to weep and wail? It was a true blessing that the horses they were asked to tend were the most magnificent Percherons. Those animals do not shy at every obstacle and sudden movement. But, dear lord," she said, returning to her place at the table, "the weeping and wailing!"

"You're being very quiet, Krista," Elaine said. "How was your day and who are these guests you say 'we' are expecting."

"My day was a strange mixture of both of yours." Krista looked at her empty bowl, waiting for the food she'd eaten to settle. "I observed but was not subjected to the masculine abuse you speak of, Elaine. Eugenie, I was tempted to – if not box ears – certainly deliver a sharp remark to weeping and wailing females." She decided she was still hungry and went to refill her bowl.

"And the guests we are expecting?" Elaine prompted.

"Andorra and what she refers to as her crew. Six women who need our help." She turned to look at her friends. "Before you ask, I have no idea of the help they need. By the time they had all six demanded, instructed, objected and whatever else they thought would get them what they wanted, I was completely confused. I used the fact that English is not even my second language and asked to be excused. I thought I had slipped through their fingers, but Andorra shouted after me that she would load the lot into her jalopy and drive over this evening. I am sorry to land you in this but you both know Andorra. There is no stopping her when she gets an idea in her head."

"I've brought bubbly and chocolates!" Andorra shouted from where she stood at the back of her group of women outside the cottage, two bottles of champagne clutched in one hand and a large box of chocolates in the other.

"Get in here!" Elaine, now dressed in a cream-and-brown outfit of slacks and jumper, almost shoved the women into the cottage. The hallway was dark, there was a war on, and the blackout was taken very seriously.

"Honestly, captain," Cox grabbed Andorra by the arm and towed her towards the open door, "you are the giddy limit!"

Eugenie stood at the back of the hall with a burning candle in her hand in an attempt to give the women unfamiliar with the cottage some light to see where they were going.

Krista was standing by the sitting-room door, waiting for the front door to close.

All three residents of the cottage felt slightly ridiculous, but this was their new way of living, and they would have to get accustomed to it – safety first.

"*Right, ladies, front and centre!*" Andorra shouted when all of the women were safely inside the sitting room. When the five women who had accompanied her stood at parade rest in front of the blacked-out window, she walked along the line, pointing and naming each individual. "Cox, Lumpy, Gnasher, Fishy and finally First." She turned on her heel. "Ladies meet Strange, Green, Wood." She wiped her hands against each other as if brushing something off. "Right, we need glasses for the bubbly. It is cold enough having been in the trunk of my jalopy." She clapped her hands. "*Chop, chop!* We have bubbly and chocolates – don't be shy!"

"May we at least sit down?" the attractive slender woman named Lumpy asked.

"It will be rather a squish." Eugenie looked around the sitting room. "This room was not designed to accommodate so many smartly uniformed individuals. If you would all remove your jackets and hats, I'll put them in the hall and perhaps we can find space to breathe."

"Here, Strange." Andorra shoved the bottles of champagne at Krista, forcing her to clutch the chilled bottles to her chest to prevent them falling to the floor. "Serve the bubbly and let us get this party started."

"I'll give you a hand." Cox was suddenly at Krista's elbow. "Lead the way."

—·ℓℓ·—

"Please forgive the captain." Cox, her uniform jacket and hat removed, stepped into the kitchen. "She's frightened. We all are but the captain is like this when we are in peril at sea. She becomes the life and soul of the party to take our minds off what we are facing. She is an amazing woman and leads from the front."

"There is no need to explain Andorra." Krista came out of the pantry, a clean linen tea towel over each shoulder, clutching empty glass jam jars. Mrs Fagin insisted the women wash the jars and keep them in the pantry in case of need. "Wood, Green and I trained with her in Portsmouth." She lowered the jam jars into the soapy water she had prepared.

"Forgive me for asking . . ." Cox watched wide eyed. "You surely don't intend to serve the best bubbly in *jam jars!*"

"There are nine of us." Krista rinsed a jar, shook the water out, took a tea towel from her shoulder and proceeded to dry the glass. She had experience, after all. "This cottage was not furnished with champagne-serving in mind." She smiled at Cox, not in the least embarrassed by failing to produce champagne flutes.

"The captain will love it." Cox pulled the spare tea towel from Krista's shoulder. "Let me give you a hand."

The nine women lounged around the sitting room. The wine and chocolate had been consumed, jokes had been made and gossip exchanged.

Krista had been waiting for one of the six women to open the dialogue, but no one seemed to be ready to speak of whatever was on their minds and it was getting late.

"Andorra." Krista stood to throw a log on the fire. "It is time."

The sudden silence in the room was almost shocking. The six visitors almost came to attention. They were no longer lounging about.

Elaine and Eugenie exchanged glances and waited.

Andorra stood and walked over to the fireplace. She turned to stare at the women who were her friends and colleagues.

"We are failing." Andorra pointed to the five women who had accompanied her. "We are all of us experienced sailors. We have had some unusual adventures that we may not discuss here. We are not accustomed to failure, but we have been forced to admit that in what has been asked of us we are failing. We have talked among ourselves and are unsure if our failure is our own fault or we are being set up to fail. We need help and that is why we are here."

"Should we be here?" Eugenie gestured between herself and Elaine.

"Who knows what you may be asked to do at some point?" Andorra sighed. "You might as well know what is in front of you. Krista, you are the only woman we know of who has been trained to undertake missions. I've spoken with Captain Waters at length, and he speaks very highly of your accomplishments. We need help."

"Where are you failing?" Krista still had no idea what these women needed from her.

"We cannot crawl through sand and muck silently, or swiftly enough," Fishy offered.

"The powers that be think our target practice is not up to much," First said. "They appear to think we should be sharpshooters."

"We are not fast enough assembling explosive packages!" Lumpy moaned.

"We are not strong enough," Gnasher said.

Krista looked from one to the other of the six women. Their upright carriage, personal grooming and cut-glass accents immediately placed them high in the upper echelons of British society. She thought of the hairy-handed, rude individuals who had prodded and cursed her through her training. Those men would not be happy if some uppity woman looked down on them. She took a deep breath, wondering how much she could say.

"Where are you receiving your training?"

Krista listened while the women proceeded to verbally annihilate every trainer and training area they had encountered. She understood their frustration, but they couldn't continue to beat their heads against so many immoveable objects.

"Andorra, I don't believe I am the best person to speak to about your troubles." Krista wanted to laugh with relief. She was going to pass this problem over to someone more qualified. "I think you need to approach Peregrine Fotheringham-Carter and his parents Admiral Sir Henry and Lady Fotheringham-Carter." She had just shifted the responsibility for these women onto Perry's shoulders. She didn't care. She had seen the effect the name of Fotheringham-Carter had on these women.

CHAPTER 8

"What have you landed me in this time?" Peregrine Fotheringham-Carter glared at Krista. He was dressed in army fatigues, his tall wide-shouldered, slim-hipped upright figure – in spite of his injured leg – shining brown hair, strong jaw, whiskey-coloured eyes and flashing dimples made him look – to Krista's eyes – like an army recruitment poster. He pushed his long-fingered hand through his hair while continuing to stare.

"Oh, hush, Perry!" Krista threw herself onto the bench seat under the window of the campervan.

She felt as if she had returned to a familiar place. The campervan Perry and she had travelled in through France, Belgium and Germany – the personal property of Captain Waters – was parked off to one side of the army training ground.

"I shot myself in the foot this time. Who knew the powers that be would insist I accompany these women?" She gestured futilely towards the exterior of the campervan. "I was trying to get them out of my hair."

"And into mine!" Perry turned the driver's seat around to face the body of the camper van and took a seat. "Thank you very much!"

Krista had missed him. It had only been a short while since they had seen each other but he had been her first friend in England. They had spent a lot of time together until war was declared.

"Seriously, Perry, I've spent the last ten days having my brain picked by those women until I am almost a blabbering idiot. When they were not demanding the details of our travel through Europe, they were discussing every move of what felt to me like every captain of the ships taking part in the Battle of the River Plate. It was an education listening to them dissect manoeuvres."

"Yes, three of our ships succeeded in at last getting rid of the *Admiral Graf Spee* which was preying on our merchant ships. Though, in fact, the *Graf Spee* was merely badly damaged, sailed away and was later scuttled by its commander to prevent it falling into British hands – after its crew were taken to Argentina. But it was a confidence boost for the navy, there is no doubt of that."

Krista tried not to roll her eyes. The men of the navy had been unbearably smug while the battle was being reported. "That was just one engagement – there will be many more to come. We need contacts with other sailors as was made clear in the battle. Where would the navy have been without the almost constant sharing of sightings of the German battleship by fishing boats and friendly nations merchant seamen? The six women I brought here today have sailing in their blood. They are well known within the sailing community. They are exactly what is needed. They are ready, willing, and able."

"So why have you dumped them on me?" Perry interrupted.

"Let us be honest here, Perry." Krista was tempted to stick out her tongue. It was so good to see him again. "I dumped them on your mother, Lady Fotheringham-Carter."

"For which Mama will not thank you." His mother was meeting with the women even as they spoke. She had agreed to share some of her own war stories with them. He was not willing to let Krista off so lightly. He had missed her. She had refused all of his invitations to dinner and was absent whenever he visited the tunnels under Dover Castle.

"Perry, as an outsider looking in …" She stopped when it looked like he might object but he only shook his head and waited for her to continue. "There are too many battles being fought clandestinely within the armed forces." She held up a hand and started counting off on her fingers. "You have the battle between the air force, army and navy which cannot be allowed to continue. You are all on the one side, for heaven's sake! Then we have the battle of the sexes. The men resent females being brought in to serve. Then we have the battle of the classes. We all bleed red, Perry …"

"Before you continue, let me assure you that you are preaching to the choir. I agree with everything you say but those battles are more than any one group can take on. We will have to approach each case as we come to it."

"I am frightened for us all, Perry." Krista stared into his beautiful thick-lashed amber eyes. "Herr Hitler has brainwashed an entire generation of the German people. They are all marching to his drum. We cannot continue to battle within our own ranks."

"One battle at a time, Krista," Perry said. "Now, tell me what you expect this camp to do for the six women you delivered here this morning."

"They are marvellous women, Perry," Krista leaned forward to say. "They have all led very adventurous lives. They have been in positions of command. One simply cannot speak down to them as if they are the village idiots." She held up a hand to stop him interrupting. "You know that is how the men in charge of training the newbies behave. You must have suffered from it yourself."

"Of course I have but I didn't complain and expect special treatment."

"Perry, I have no great knowledge of what these women have been recruited to do." Krista had made some guesses from what the women had and hadn't said. "They have all volunteered for missions that, if I am not very much mistaken, could be considered suicide missions. They deserve to receive the best training we can give them. They should be given the best chance of surviving."

"Come on, you lot!" the harsh male voice shouted. *"Follow our little foreign flower here! Move it!"*

Krista grimaced and continued to crawl using her elbows and knees to move her body along the cold wet ground. The women were covering an obstacle course set up for the army. Thankfully there were no male observers shouting abuse at them. None, that is, except the man she had requested be their trainer. Master Sergeant Wilbur Hemp was a veritable martinet, but the man got things done and he hadn't a malicious bone in his body.

"Fishy, you're not swimming in the ocean now! Dig those elbows in and slide along the ground! Cox, you are not supposed to be dining on the muck! Come on now, you little daffodils – move it! I'd like to get home before supper is on the table! Move it!"

The seven women had been run over obstacles. They had been barked at when they tried to assist each other over difficult places in the course. The sergeant had been tipped the wink that their missions would be solitary. There would be no-one to help them when they were out in the field. They were sending women out to do a man's job and he would be fried if they did not receive the best training he could give them.

"Come on now, my little daffodils!" Hemp walked along, watching every move the women made. *"You're going to love this next lot! It will remind you of those mud baths I hear you fancy ladies pay a fortune for!"* He continued to shout and move them along.

The women followed his every order. There was no moaning, no whimpering, no back-talk. They were silent, determined to learn all that they could.

~~eee~~

"I swear that muck got under my clothing and into places that have never been touched before." Cox put her head under the warm water running from the shower.

"Who has the shampoo?" Gnasher demanded.

"Be grateful for hot water," Fish remarked.

The seven women were standing naked in an open shower block set aside for their use this evening. They had gratefully stripped out of their mucky clothing and into the showers.

"Your advice on clothing was much appreciated, Strange." Andorra scrubbed frantically at her hair, trying to remove every last vestige of muck. "Those waterproof overalls you suggested we buy are marvellous. Are we supposed to launder our own things ourselves?"

"When you're out in the field," Krista was trying to pass along as much information as she could, "the last thing on your mind will be clean laundry, I assure you. However, when you get covered in wet muck as we did this evening, I suggest you allow the muck to dry and then brush it off to the best of your ability."

"Where on earth did you find that man Hemp, Strange?" First examined her arm, unsure if a mark was a bruise or muck. She continued to scrub while waiting for a response.

"Master Sergeant Wilbur Hemp is that rare article, ladies, a true gent." Krista closed her eyes and allowed the hot water to run over her. "I want you all to take him out for a drink. I don't suggest you get him drunk. That would cost an absolute fortune. The man has a hollow leg where drink is concerned. However, away from the base he has stories that will make your hair curl. Those stories hold pearls of wisdom that you would be foolish to ignore."

"What kind of stories?" Lumpy asked.

"The sergeant has a relative – I am unsure if it was his father or grandfather . . ." Krista sluiced the water down her body. She stepped out of the shower onto the concrete floor. She used a large rough towel to dry herself while continuing to speak. "This relative ran away from home to join the Wild West Show that travelled through Britain at the end of the last century. He learned the most amazing things from people like the legendary Annie Oakley and the American Indians who travelled with the show. Listen to his stories, ladies, and treat every word that falls from his lips as a pearl of wisdom."

"You jest, Strange!" Andorra stepped out onto the concrete and joined Krista.

"Not in the least, captain." Krista had fallen into the habit of calling Andorra 'captain' as the other women did. "I know nothing about sailing and would never dare to even comment on matters of seamanship. Sergeant Hemp told me his stories over a pint while Perry and I were in training here. I listened and applied some of what he had said to the exercises we were given. The sergeant noticed and continued to help me. I am praying he will do the same for you ladies. If you sneer or doubt him, he will train you in the fashion that is mandated by the armed forces. You will undoubtedly pass the tests at the end of your time here, but you will have failed in his eyes and indeed in mine."

"Give us one example," Cox said.

All of the women were standing on the concrete floor now. The water had been turned off and every woman was listening intently.

Krista began dressing while trying to think of just one example of the wisdom the sergeant had passed along to Perry and herself.

Soon they were all dressed and sitting on the bench that stretched the length of the shower room, each woman wearing navy slacks and jumpers, bending forward to don their shoes and socks.

Krista had thought of a telling example to give them. "Andorra has mentioned the problems the Wrens are having passing the navy's shooting tests."

They all began to grumble about the horrors of failing at something they considered themselves skilled in.

Krista continued. "Have you ever played Cowboys and Indians?"

"Oh now, really, Strange!" Fishy snapped. "Of course we have, hasn't everyone?"

"Ladies," Krista needed them to hear what she was saying, "Sergeant Hemp will train you on the proper use and care of your firearm. In fact, he will be so demanding that you will be tempted to either hit him over the head with a gun or shoot him. The man's a demanding taskmaster." She finished tying her shoelaces and stood to stare at the women sitting on the bench. "*Are you listening to me?*" she demanded and waited until they were all looking at her.

"Do get on with it, Strange!" Andorra leaned back and waited.

"Master Sergeant Hemp will not waste ammunition so what I strongly suggest you ladies do is purchase a box of ammunition – with your own money – and bring it with you to the firing range." She looked from one woman to another. "Then nicely ask the master sergeant to demonstrate his sharpshooting skills. It will be an eye-opener. The man's a legend on the firing range. Learn from him. I did and I have never regretted it."

Krista had done all that she could. She had given these women she had come to admire the best chance of succeeding at their tasks. It was up to them now to put any prejudice they might have to one side and listen to a man who, while not being in the same social class as themselves, stood head and shoulders above them in Krista's regard.

CHAPTER 9

"Your Wrens appear to be hanging on Master Sergeant Hemp's every word." Perry put a pint of bitter and a glass of shandy on the tabletop.

The Grouse and Hen, a public house close to the army training grounds, was packed with warm bodies sitting and standing around. A pall of smoke from the many cigarettes hung in the air. Perry and Krista were sitting at a table for two, pushed back against a wall. The six Wrens Krista brought to the base were in the company of the grizzled master sergeant at several small tables pushed close and pulled to one side of the log-burning fire in the inglenook. The noise from that area was attracting the attention of many of the army men.

"Here comes another one!" Krista watched a soldier approach the tables. It had become a spectator sport to see the young men approach the group with a spring in their step, hoping to be invited to share the table with the beauties surrounding the master sergeant.

"There goes another one!" Perry laughed behind his pint of bitter. He nudged his spindle-legged chair around so he faced Krista. "Should I be flattered that you chose to sit to one side with me?"

"We have both heard the good master sergeant's stories already." Krista sipped her shandy. The drink was mostly lemonade with a little beer added to cut the sweetness. She'd been introduced to the drink by Perry the first time she'd visited an English public house. "I believe the man deserves the undivided attention of the women he has taken in hand. The women need to understand that when the master sergeant asks something of them, he is an expert in his field. That is vital. The sergeant has a great deal to teach them and they must be willing to learn."

"Let us leave them to their business," Perry said. "I want to speak with you. We haven't had a chance to really speak in some time. I was about to give you a telephone call and ask what you are doing over the holidays."

"The holidays!" Krista almost groaned. She fought the temptation to hit her head off the table. "I have heard of nothing else from my two roommates. Reggie is issuing passes for them to return home. To hear Elaine and Eugenie speak you'd think they had been away from home for years."

"There is no possibility of you returning to France. Where are you intending to spend the holiday period?" He had spoken to his mother about inviting Krista to his home for the holidays. His mother had advised against the idea. Christmas was a time for family and inviting a stranger – particularly an attractive female – into their family celebrations would be very uncomfortable for Krista. She would be interrogated ceaselessly by his older brothers and their wives. He had been disappointed but saw the wisdom in his mother's words.

"I don't believe I will be free over the holidays." Krista would never have returned to Metz and the Dumas family, even if such a thing were possible. Her memories of her time spent with the people claiming to be her family were not pleasant. She had been planning her escape from their less than loving care even before she was forced to flee. "To my knowledge I am to remain available to Reggie." She sipped her drink for a moment. "I was wondering if you knew where Philippe is stationed?" The man she considered her brother, Philippe Dumas – as far as she knew was in the same clandestine group as Perry.

Perry smiled. "Have I ever thanked you for introducing me to him? He has become quite the feather in my cap, I can tell you."

"How so?" She noticed he hadn't answered her question.

"Thanks to you I was able to bring Philippe to the attention of my superiors – he is considered in some small way my protégé." He shrugged. "Which is ridiculous as I have stated time and again. However, the man brought information and connections with him that have enabled my superiors to increase their knowledge of the ground forces in Europe. The information Philippe shared is proving very useful to them."

"You two are being very anti-social."

The pair jumped. They hadn't noticed Andorra approaching their table on her way to the toilets.

"What are you drinking?" Andorra put a hand on Krista's shoulder and leaned in slightly. "It is my turn to buy a round of drinks."

"Are you slightly squiffy there, captain?" Perry thought the lady was well on her way to being drunk. "I would advise against trying to outdrink the good master sergeant."

"I am, I believe," Andorra weaved slightly on her feet, "more tired than drunk. I have pains in parts of my body I never knew I possessed. This one," she hit Krista's shoulder, "and the fiend she put in charge of us have quite exhausted me."

"Why don't I find a driver to take you back to the base?" Perry pushed away from the table. "You have more drills early in the morning." He didn't want to even think about them trying to pass the master sergeant's tests after a late night and too much to drink. That was a disaster in the making. Also, if they left now, it would spare him from answering Krista's questions about her brother.

"Capital idea." Andorra nodded and regretted it. "Krista, are you ready to leave?"

"It's time we all left," Krista responded.

She walked across to join the Wrens, suggesting they quickly finish their drinks.

Krista made sure the women had their belongings with them and they visited the public house toilets while Perry sought out one of the ferry drivers to take them back to the base. There was much good-humoured shouting and laughter while the women took their leave of the pub. The off-colour shouts and suggestions to the driver of the ferry – a canvas-covered lorry – were stopped by a barked order and a glare from Master Sergeant Hemp.

"Someone shoot that bugler!" Andorra groaned.

"It is time to be up and about." Krista rolled from the cot she'd slept in, glad to leave the thin mattress stretched over the wire cot. She had spent a most uncomfortable night.

"Someone shoot Strange!" Andorra pushed her face into the thin pillow.

"*Ladies!*" Krista's handclap made more than one woman groan and curse. "I will be leaving you today."

"*What!*" Andorra, her face lined by a seam from the rough pillow, glared at Krista. "You are leaving us here at the mercy of those hairy-handed louts?"

"Why are you being excused from duty?" Cox stood by the side of her cot.

The women had been granted a Nissan hut for their barracks. A line of cots stretched lengthwise along each side of the hut. There was a metal chest at the foot of each bed for storage. There were more cots than there were women. A free-standing fireplace – cold now – stood at the opposite end of the hut from the door.

"I have already passed Master Sergeant Hemp's tests, thank you very much." Krista was pulling her pyjamas from her shivering body as she spoke. "You lot need to be up, dressed and have order restored to the barracks before you head into the main building for breakfast." She pushed her pyjamas into her haversack which sat in the open chest at the foot of her cot.

"Cox!" Andorra whimpered.

"Sorry, Captain." Cox was pulling clothes on. "I am one of the men now. No special dispensation for you, I'm afraid. Up and at 'em!"

"Someone remind me why I ever signed up for this lot?" Andorra, still moaning, left her cot. "If we are to stay here for any length of time, we need to be better prepared. I am not willing to shiver and shake all night long then arise to freezing cold conditions. It is past bearing."

"We were all a mite too merry to think about lighting that fire last night." Lumpy was dressed and making her cot.

"We will need to gather fuel." Fishy stood by her cot. "I could swear I crawled over half a forest of broken branches yesterday. We should begin a stockpile as we go, I think. I too am not fond of shivering and shaking."

"You ladies can make plans over breakfast." Krista was dressed, her haversack packed and her cot stripped. "You will have to work together to make your – I hesitate to call them living quarters – comfortable."

"I will see what I can scrounge by way of kettle, cups and such while we are out and about," Cox offered. "But I will not be keeping that fireplace stocked and lit."

Discussing matters that needed to be attended to, the women restored order to the hut and when all was in order they stood before the door to the outside world, gathered their composure and sallied forth to face another day of training.

"You have got your chicks off, I see." Perry put his cup and saucer on the tabletop across from where Krista sat alone at one of the tables in the canteen. "What are your plans?"

"I'm waiting for a ferry to take me back to Dover." Krista thought about going to the counter for another cup of tea but decided she'd had enough for the moment.

"I would like to take you out to dinner one evening." Perry wanted to spend time alone without responsibilities with Krista. It was difficult to find a time when they were both free.

"I always enjoy your company, Perry." Krista smiled. "Why don't you telephone the cottage. I don't know what my duties will be in the coming days."

"I have received my orders . . ." Perry checked their surroundings. The canteen was practically empty thankfully. The men and women based at the camp had already eaten and were about their duties. "You and I are to be sent out as a mixed forces team."

"I've heard nothing of this."

"You and I are to be assigned together in the week between Christmas and the New Year. I believe, and it is only my best guess, mind, but I believe that is why the campervan has been left on site. I think they plan for us to use it again."

"Do tell!" Krista pushed her cup and saucer away before leaning in closer.

"Have you heard of ships being sighted off the coast, ships that are thought to be picking up people of interest to the Crown?" Perry's lips almost didn't move as he spoke.

"No."

"The local fishermen have noticed unfamiliar boats out on the ocean when they engage in night fishing." Perry couldn't tell Krista that it was her brother Philippe's contacts that had brought the matter to the attention of the powers that be. "There have even been reports of submarine sightings in our waters."

"I hadn't heard." Krista wasn't surprised she had heard nothing of the matter. People were beginning to be very careful about what they said – and where they said it – which was a good thing, in her opinion.

"Rear Admiral Andrews – Reggie to you – is aware of the situation. He has been in talks with Captain Waters about the matter. Do you fancy another mug of tea?" Perry suddenly asked when a service man appeared at his shoulder to clear the table.

"That would be lovely." Krista nodded to the serviceman, pushing her mug in his direction

Perry stood and walked towards the service counter.

Krista sat back in her chair and waited.

Perry placed the two mugs of tea he'd carried onto the tabletop. "I'll telephone you at the cottage."

"The line is not secure." Krista took the mug of tea, wrapping her hands around the thick porcelain for warmth.

"I am aware." Perry grimaced.

The entrance of a ferry driver looking for Krista put an end to any conversation they might have. With a smile of regret Perry stood and watched as Krista, her haversack over one shoulder, hurried after the driver.

CHAPTER 10

December 24th

1939

"Here, put this on you." Marie Fagin, her head of grey curls covered by a headscarf wrapped in turban fashion, held out a blue cotton wraparound apron. "I don't know what those two friends of yours were thinking of – imagine not even inviting you to their homes for Christmas!"

"They were so excited at the chance to go home for Christmas." Krista laughed while she pushed her arms through the sleeveless garment, crossing the sides around her body before tightening the cotton strings around her waist twice. "They never gave my plans a thought."

Elaine and Eugenie had been like whirling dervishes when they received their pass. Krista had not been able to keep up with their many shouted orders and requests as they prepared to return to their homes for what many believed would be the last peaceful Christmas for years. She had helped her two friends where she could, but they had almost run from the cottage in their frantic dash to the train station.

"They were like overexcited children."

"That is no excuse!" Marie Fagin snapped.

"Mam, will you give it a rest, please?" Franny Fagin, her blonde hair escaping from her turban headscarf, said. "Krista is going to think you don't want her here."

"Devil a bit of it!" Marie glared.

The Fagin women plus Krista were in the kitchen of the Fagins' cottage, peeling vegetables and pre-preparing as much of the work needed to serve Christmas dinner next day to the small herd that Marie had invited to her home for the seasonal celebration. Krista admired the way the women were able to ignore the shouts, thumps, and noise coming from the children gathered in the living room.

"Mrs Fagin, will you really need that many potatoes?" Krista looked at the small mountain of potatoes that Marie was peeling with a speed and skill that was impressive. The bare white peeled potatoes were being put in buckets of clear salted water,

"I'd rather have too much than too little." Marie continued to remove the potatoes' skins.

"The men of the household have hearty appetites," Sheila Fagin, Mrs Fagin's daughter-in-law, said softly while attending to the Brussels sprouts. "The children have little bottomless pits for stomachs."

"I'm that grateful to the neighbours that keep me supplied with fresh vegetables from their gardens." Mrs Fagin swept her arms around the table covered in various muck-covered vegetables. "I would have to spend a fortune at the greengrocer's to buy this lot, I can tell you," She waved the knife she was using for peeling at the women gathered around the heavy wooden kitchen table. "And I'll tell you this much for nothing, no greengrocer would have such beautiful fresh produce." She nodded her head, sending her turban scarf over her eyes. She pushed the scarf back in place with a muck-covered hand.

"According to the Ministry of Agriculture," Franny was pulling heads of cabbage apart before dropping the leaves into the bucket of salted water at her feet, "we will soon be turning every inch of earth into vegetable gardens. I've seen the posters for their 'Digging for Britain' scheme."

"They had better not come around here counting every potato we pull out of the ground!" Marie Fagin never took her eyes from her work. "What with planning to ration every little thing we put in our mouth and fill out forms for everything under the sun, I don't know what the world's coming to!" She sighed deeply. "I do miss those Frenchmen visiting and selling their onions and garlic. Not that I'm that fond of garlic, mind you, but I do love a good onion."

Frenchmen on heavy black bicycles, a beret titled dashingly to the sides of their heads, had long been a familiar sight riding around the streets of Kent and surrounding counties selling strings of onions and garlic. That trade had ceased at the outbreak of war.

"You can't beat those big moist sweet French onions. Our home-grown are never as good, I don't care what anyone says," Sheila Fagin said. "You can't beat an onion for adding a bit of flavour."

Krista, peeling carrots, had no idea what the women were talking about but enjoyed listening and sharing in the work.

"Still," Marie said, "mustn't grumble."

"I've finished the cabbage, Mammy." Franny wiped her hands on her wraparound apron. "Will I put the bucket outside the back door?"

"You will not! I don't trust next-door's dog not to knock over the buckets." Marie stopped her peeling for a moment. "That article puts its nose into everything. We'll put the vegetables in the garden shed out of harm's way. The geese are hanging by the neck in the pantry."

"He won't be able to keep that dog," Sheila said. "Not with a war on."

"We'll not be the ones to tell any nosy government man that he has a dog." Marie glared at her daughter-in-law. "It's none of our never mind."

"*Mammy!*"

Sheila was almost knocked off her feet when her four-year-old daughter Lily charged into the kitchen and threw her arms around her mother's legs.

"Peter won't make me a paper hat!" the little girl wailed.

"I'm not making her another one!" Six-year-old Peter stormed into the kitchen, his chin leading the way. He stood with arms crossed over his knitted sleeveless vest and glared. "She keeps tearing them up!"

"Now, you children did such a lovely job making the paper chains and blowing up the balloons to decorate my room." Marie knew she'd get no peace with children under her feet. "Santa Claus will be coming down the chimney tonight. You don't want him to hear the pair of you behaving like little hooligans, do you?"

"No, Nanny." Peter dropped his chin.

"I'll put the kettle on." Marie matched words to action.

Krista let herself into her dark cottage. She'd been invited to join the adult Fagins in a drink and a sing-along. She had never experienced a day like it. So many people coming and going. The neighbours and their overexcited children running in and out of the house. The adults with worried frowns. The Battle of the Plate, the sea battle fought and won that month, might have made for exciting times, but it was also a worrying taste of things to come. The adults worked hard at keeping their worries from the children. All of them had friendly inquisitive questions about her.

She did not remove her heavy coat but hurried into the front room and poked at the embers in the fireplace. She had drawn the blackout curtains before she left the house and covered the fire with wet slack to keep it smouldering while she was away. A few sticks over the embers and soon bright flames were warming her face and hands. She added some small pieces of coal to the flames before practically falling into one of the fireside chairs, dropping her head tiredly against the chair back.

"It is dangerous to leave your key hanging from a string at the back of the door," a masculine voice said into the darkness.

"*Nom de Dieu!*" Krista swore, her hand flailing for the light-switch on the lamp on the table next to the chair she was sitting in. She'd recognised the voice – thankfully. "Philippe Dumas, what are you doing here?" She threw herself out of her chair in his direction. She pressed kisses into his cheek, her arms tight around his shoulders.

A dark-haired, dark-eyed man struggled to push himself into a sitting position on the sofa. He laughed softly while returning her embrace.

"I came to visit my little sister," Philippe said in French. "That is not a crime."

Philippe had grown up believing the tall white-haired, blue-eyed beauty was his sister. That was despite the fact that members of the Dumas family were short in stature with dark hair and dark-brown eyes. His parents stated that Krista was his sister. Who was he to doubt that? It was only as he matured that he questioned that fact.

"Have you eaten?" Krista almost closed her eyes in despair at her own words. Really, she had not seen her brother for what seemed like ages and the first thing she asked was if he had eaten? But she was trying to accept the evidence of her eyes. Philippe sleeping on her sofa – what a surprise!

"You did not smell the onions and garlic when you came through the door?" Philippe put one arm around her shoulders and stared. "You will have to be more alert than this, little sister – we all have to be aware of the world around us if we are to survive the madness that is surrounding us."

"What are you doing here, Phillippe? How did you get here?" The last she had been aware of this brother he'd been involved in hush-hush manoeuvres within the armed forces.

"I travelled to Dover with a companion." Phillippe ran his hand through his hair, sighing deeply and staring into her familiar blue eyes. "I needed a taste of sanity. Something or someone from home who carried only pleasant memories. I have spent the last twenty months fighting a war that no one was willing to admit was real. Now, we are facing a monster and his army, and we are not ready. You would think the navy had won the war in this last month. The Battle of the Plate. *Bah!*" He gave a gallic shrug. "I could not join in the festivities surrounding me."

"The recent battle at sea has given the navy a great boost in morale. It would appear you need such a boost yourself, big brother." Krista pulled her legs up onto the sofa.

Her move caused Philippe to drop his arm and allowed her to make a visual examination of his features.

There was silence while she waited for him to speak. When it looked as if she'd have to prompt him, she asked, "What's wrong, Philippe?" She had grown up with this man. He had always been her favourite of her three older Dumas brothers. "You look dreadful, you have bags under your eyes I could use for packing cases. What is bothering you?"

"Nightmares," he answered without adding a word of explanation.

"We have both seen dreadful things ..." She had never shared with him the things she had seen in Germany.

"I can't close my eyes without seeing the images, Krista," Philippe said.

"Why don't you tell me about it?"

"I don't want to put those images in your mind, Krista." He raised his hip off the sofa to search in his trouser pocket for his cigarettes and lighter.

He lit up and puffed heavily on the cigarette, watching the smoke float towards the ceiling before saying. "Sometimes I believe I am going mad."

"Tell me."

The only sound in the room for some time was the crackling of the coal in the fire.

Krista waited. Philippe would tell her, or he would not. It was his choice.

"Do you remember when I returned to the Auberge that morning?" He stood to throw the butt of his cigarette into the fire. "The morning I left …" He appeared to fall into his dark memories.

"How could I not? It was a day that changed both of our lives," she whispered. "I have relived my memories of that dreadful day so many times."

He returned to the sofa and gave a bitter laugh. "In my dreams I am always a hero instead of the craven coward I really am. Good God, Krista – how could they do it – how could men I had grown up with and around – some of whom I'd admired – how could they behave in such a dreadful manner? They behaved like depraved animals. No, they are worse than any beast in the animal kingdom."

"Hanna …" Krista's mind made the leap. Her friend's mother was of the Jewish faith. The children were being raised in that faith. They had been hounded out of their village on that fateful day. She closed her eyes, praying that Hanna was not the subject of her brother's nightmares.

"Yes, indeed, Hanna Charleston." Philippe raised one hip and dug deep into his trouser pocket again. "I admired her, you know – my precious Hanna – we knew her family would prefer she consort with a man of the Jewish faith, but we were friends – always." His hands, holding a cigarette and lighter, shook as he tried to light a cigarette. He finally succeeded in putting a flame to the end of his cigarette. He inhaled an enormous mouthful of smoke, his chest expanding before allowing the smoke to escape his pursed lips while he watched the snake of smoke appear in the air before him.

Hanna Charleston and her family had owned the boulangerie in the village of Metz. She had been a friend to Krista and obviously something more to Philippe. The day before Krista had been forced to escape from her home, Hanna and her family had been forced from their home and business by some of Hitler's thugs.

"They killed them, you know – all of them." There was moisture in Philippe's dark eyes.

"No, no, you are mistaken, Philippe," Krista sat forward to say. "Yes, they forced them from their home and business. I knew that and was ashamed I could do nothing to help but they left in their big van – you know, the one they used for deliveries."

"They left the village of Metz in that big bakery delivery van." Philippe sucked on his cigarette. "Yes, indeed, how merciful!" He glared through the smoke at Krista, tears running freely down his face. "I saw them, Krista. I was too far away to offer help. I hid behind a tree trunk, not understanding anything." He shook his head. "I have relived that scene so many times. There was nothing I could do. They lined them up, Krista . . ." He fell into his memories.

Krista was incapable of speaking, just stared at her brother as he fought to control his emotions.

"They had beaten and abused Hanna, her mother, and sisters. I could tell," he bit out between clenched teeth. "They trembled before those big strong men." He would not mention that they were all naked. "So proud of themselves as they laughed and held guns on the innocent." Still sitting on the sofa, he threw his half-smoked cigarette into the grate before burying his face in his hands.

Krista had taken solace from knowing that her friend and her family had safely left the village in their van. She had thought to meet up someday with Hanna and discover all of her news. How had it come to this?

"Philippe," she said when his shoulders stopped shaking and he drew a deep breath, "where did this happen?"

"The Jourdan farm."

"*No!*"

"Oh, but yes! I watched as the oh-so-charming Guillaume Jourdan sat waiting in one of those smoke-belching beasts of a farm machine. There was a long deep ditch he must have prepared in advance."

"I would never have believed it of Guillaume Jourdan." Krista closed her eyes against the images trying to form in her head.

"They had to hold the father and brothers upright. They had been so badly beaten I don't even know if they were conscious. Perhaps that was a mercy. They shot them, Krista, those men we knew – they shot the innocent and laughed. They joked as they wiped out an entire family."

The image of his friends, neighbours and some members of his own family behaving in such a way had frozen him to the spot. It was over in a matter of moments but in his nightmares it took hours, giving him time to react – to change the fate of the Charleston family in some way. But he had cowered behind a tree – what could he do except die? – he was a glorified waiter watching hell visit his world.

"They used that family as landfill, Krista, and I could only watch." He bowed his head and sobbed. Guillaume had used his farm machine to fill in the ditch then those same 'brave' men danced and urinated on the mass grave, still laughing, while he himself bent over and emptied his stomach until he collapsed.

Krista put her arm around his trembling shoulders and he collapsed against her. He sobbed into her shoulder while she held him. She was unaware of the tears running down her own face as she stared sightlessly into the fire.

CHAPTER 11

"Did you sleep?" Krista yawning, wearing her pyjamas under her heavy woollen dressing gown, turned to greet Philippe when he stumbled into the kitchen the following morning. It was Christmas Day. She had the fire started in the range and was standing in front of the flames, enjoying the warmth.

"Strangely enough, I did." He rasped his hand across the dark stubble on his chin. "Your sofa is very comfortable and the warmth from the fire was welcome. However, the silence of the night and the lack of sweaty snoring men surrounding me almost kept me awake."

"I did offer you the use of one of the beds upstairs."

"I could not add to your work. In this weather getting sheets and bedding laundered must be a nightmare. I was perfectly comfortable on the sofa."

"So speaks the son of an innkeeper!" Krista laughed. "I know of no other man who would worry about changing bedding!"

"I was – how do they say – 'snug as a bug in a rug'," he said in a mixture of French and English. He kissed her on each cheek in the French fashion. "Did you sleep?" He would have thought the conversation last night would not be conducive to a good night's sleep. He regretted sharing his memories with her but had needed to speak of the horrors he'd seen to someone who would understand his pain.

"We were, both of us, emotionally exhausted." Her own mind had mercifully shut down in the small hours of the morning, allowing her to get some much-needed sleep. She reached for her coffee carafe and held it aloft. "I have just enough coffee grounds for one pot of coffee. I am offering to share my treasure with you, brother. I hope you are suitably honoured."

"Where is my head?" Philippe slapped his own forehead. "Where did I leave my haversack?" He turned and left the kitchen. He was back in moments with a well-stuffed haversack in hand. He threw it on top of the kitchen table. "Make the coffee by all means, sister dear, I could use a cup of strong dark coffee to start my day." He began taking items from the depths of the bag.

Krista watched, her eyes growing wide, as he removed item after item that were almost impossible to get in the shops. He held two pounds of coffee aloft, one in each hand while he smiled at her. He put the packets of ground coffee on the table.

"There is no point leaving this tin of the best Russian black caviar for you, is there?" he said, laughing as he held it aloft.

"No." She scrunched her nose. "I detest the stuff."

"Peasant."

"Where did you get all of these things, Philippe?" She waved her hands about as more items were removed from the bag. Sugar and was that a tin of ham?

"I and several others liberated them from a German forces supply convoy," he said offhandedly. "The Germans had no more need of the food."

Krista simply stared without speaking, desperately trying not to think of the terror involved in attacking a company of Germans. She would not ask for details. Truthfully, she really didn't want to know. They would all have to do things that they had never conceived of before the world had given in to madness. Her brother was a long way from the laughing, cheerful waiter he once was. She picked up a packet of coffee grounds in each hand and sniffed luxuriously. She was not about to refuse this treasure. She put the coffee back on the table before turning back to the stove.

"Would you care for something to eat?" She wasn't sure what she had in the pantry but she could give him something even if only a slice of fried bread and an egg. Mrs Fagin, bless her, had a friend who kept chickens so a regular supply of eggs was available to them – for the moment – there was talk of restricting such free trade.

"Thank you but no."

"We have a gas water-heater in the bathroom upstairs if you want to shave and freshen up while the coffee percolates."

"Hot water, I do not know if I can use such luxury anymore." He searched the haversack to insure he had removed all of the treasure. Only the lone tin of caviar remained inside. It would be dangerous to take it with him. He raised the tin in the air and with a loud thump placed it on the table. "I'll leave the caviar – one never knows, you may have a guest with discerning taste sometime. I cannot take it with me."

"You could always eat it." She knew how much he loved the little black fish eggs.

"Without ceremony and the proper accompaniments?" He gazed at her in mock horror. "Where did we go wrong in raising you? You are a true peasant."

"And proud of it!" She laughed. Her distaste for caviar was truly baffling to her French family. But why force yourself to eat something that made you cringe? No matter how sophisticated it was thought to be!

"I've been invited next door for Christmas dinner with the Fagin family," Krista said.

They were sitting at the kitchen table enjoying their second pot of coffee – washed and dressed for the day.

"I am sure Mrs Fagin wouldn't mind setting another place at the table." She smiled. "Lord knows, I think she has invited the street to eat."

"Dry goose and overcooked vegetables!" Philippe grimaced.

"Snob."

"I thank you for the invitation – second-hand though it be – but I have to leave soon. I have a boat to catch." It would soon be too dangerous to openly travel over the Channel. The powers that be were working on travel plans between England and the continent. He stifled a sigh. He was here in Krista's kitchen, enjoying the time spent with the woman he would always think of as his sister. One had to grab at these occasions of sanity where one found them.

"Any time you have contraband to unload, please feel free to visit!" Krista was trying desperately to remain light-hearted. She did not have to be told her brother was going into danger. She understood that his underground work was valued but she was sure he took too many chances with his life. Just listening to him speak had given her the impression that he was living very much for the moment. She was happy that he had taken the time to visit her.

"You know, it was your friend Perry who suggested I visit you." Philippe noticed her sorrow but what could he do? He had joined the fight against terror and would not turn his back on his people or his country.

"It was nice of Perry to suggest that. I have missed you."

"He is frustrated and longs to join the fighting forces," Philippe said simply. It did not do to talk openly of current affairs. "I have told him often and true that he serves a needed purpose. The son of a naval admiral serving in the armed forces. They do not know what to do with him. His family connections appear to be many and varied. He is a good man."

Krista waited. She knew her brother. He had something further to say.

"Krista, my sister, do not let them send you into Europe." He sipped his coffee, trying to force his throat open. He was terrified for her. "There is talk – at the highest level – of using you to spy in Europe. Do not let them send you into that madhouse. I beg of you. I know of your parentage now. I am happy you were able to discover the truth about your birth. You come from the nobility which I find hard to believe because of your peasant palate!" They shared a laughing glance. "But listen to me well, my sister. These English, they do not allow you to enlist. You are a free agent. Please, if they request you to travel to Europe – decline – most forcefully."

"I have already refused to become a spy." She would not allow Clarence Brownlow-Hastings to turn her into something she never wanted to become. "What do you know that I don't?" She reached across the table and put her hand on top of his clenched fist. "What has you so worried?"

"It is a horror." Philippe closed his eyes against the images that tried to form in his mind. "Some of it you will know. After all, have we not been listening to the gossip coming out of Germany for years? We were well placed in Metz, on the border between France and Germany, to pick up a lot of stories we thought were horrible fantasies – 'drink talking' as it were. Sadly we have been able to confirm that such stories are true. Hitler's forces have been snatching children off the streets of neighbouring countries for years. We have heard the mutterings and rumours, have we not? Blond-haired blue-eyed children, they steal them, Krista, and put them into institutions where they learn to be good soldiers for the Reich. But that is not all they have done." He opened his fist and captured her fingers. "They take women too. It does not matter if they want to go but they try first to entice them. If that does not work, they use force, and none stand against them. German males who meet the physical standards for the new Germany are encouraged to visit these houses. These houses are there for birthing the future soldiers of the Reich. I have seen them, Krista, and my sister – you are just the kind of woman they seek."

"I know." For years there had been rumblings in Metz of disappearances and these houses where women were kept prisoner to serve as breeding mares for the Fatherland.

"You know!" He threw her hand away from him, shoved back his chair and stood glaring down at her. "You know and you let me spill my guts!"

"Sit down, Philippe." Krista waved at his chair. "I have known of these houses for some time now. It was all the women whispered about in Metz. Your father too knew of these houses." She couldn't meet his eyes. "He gave me to Maurice La Flange – for his entertainment. Maurice offered me the honour of servicing him or my entrance into one of those houses."

"*Pigs!*" Philippe spat as he sat.

"It is the main reason I fled France. Why would I want to return and find myself in that same situation? The very thought makes my flesh creep."

"Do you not miss home?" He could not imagine being unable to return to France. It was his home – his country.

"What home?" She waited a moment. "Forgive me, but I never felt as if I belonged in the Dumas family."

"And you belong here?" He waved his arms about.

"I do not know where I belong." She sighed. "I do not want you to think I am feeling sorry for myself. I miss France, how could I not? It is all I ever knew until I came to England. But I knew even as I fled that I must make a life for myself here. The war – as it has for many – has derailed any plans I might have made. Now, now I simply live each day as it comes. But I live and I have found a purpose."

"What is it the English say?" Philippe smiled. "'Mustn't grumble'."

"They do have some wonderful sayings." Krista was happy to see the smile return to his face. "We are more fortunate than a great many, Philippe."

"So we are, my sister."

They sat in silence for a moment, each wondering when they would see each other again but neither daring to say the words.

"Thank you for the bed and breakfast."

"What breakfast – coffee? You refused food."

"I have a boat to catch and I am afraid I am not a good sailor." He grimaced to think of what lay ahead of him. He was one of those unfortunates that hung over the side as soon as he stepped on board ship.

"Landlubber!" Krista didn't suffer from *mal de mer* but she could sympathise.

"One does what one must." He stood and simply stared at her for a moment. "Take care of yourself."

"It was good to see you." Krista stood, shoving her chair back.

She walked beside him, watching him collect his belongings, trying to store the image of him in her mind and heart. Who knew when they would meet again? She followed him to the door, holding it open while he stepped out into the cold morning mist.

It was an awkward leave-taking. What could one say under the circumstances? Stay safe? Take care? Where was safe in these troubled times? So she fell back on what she knew. She kissed his cheeks, perhaps adding more pressure than the normal polite brush of the lips. She wished him *bonne chance* and *au revoir*.

CHAPTER 12

December 26th

1939

Krista pulled off her padded leather driving gloves. She removed her helmet, tearing strands of her hair out at the same time. She didn't remove her jacket. The house was cold. She resisted – barely – slamming the door of the cottage with enough force to crack the wood and glass. She put her gloves in her helmet before throwing them towards the stairs, smiling with satisfaction when they landed neatly on a stair-tread. She would take them upstairs when she went. She'd just returned from an early morning meeting with Rear Admiral Andrews. She'd left the meeting almost choking on the angry words she'd longed to let loose.

"I cannot believe the powers that be expect me to sit on top of a cliff in a campervan!" she shouted aloud to the empty cottage. "Wear a pretty dress, he says! Well, darn you, Reggie, have you any idea of the wild winds that blow along those very clifftops? I will freeze my nether regions off. I'll bet no one told Perry to wear a blessed dress!" She unstrapped the shin-guards she wore to protect the legs of her slacks before removing her ankle boots.

She didn't want to walk muck through the cottage. In thick woollen socks, she stood for a moment battling her emotions.

She wanted to kick something. The last two days had been difficult for her. Seeing her brother, listening to his tales of horror, had left her emotionally off balance. She'd gone to the Fagin house with a smile on her face – she had to. To pretend to be light-hearted when she'd joined the Fagin family around the Christmas table. She'd joined in the games and laughter. She hadn't been the only one there forcing a simulation of good humour. She longed for time to herself. Time to think or did she mean dwell on her misery?

"I want a pot of coffee." She knew she was being ridiculous but there was no one here to witness her snit. "I want to scream the house down. I don't want to sit on top of a cliff pretending to be Perry's mistress for the entertainment of any who might be listening. The powers that be are insane!"

The telephone on the hall table began to peal before she reached the kitchen. She dropped her head, clenched her fists, and fought to rein in her temper. If that was Reggie telephoning to reprimand her for her insolence, she had to remain calm.

"Hello." She gave the telephone number and waited.

"Darling ..." said a male voice.

It was Perry. She took a deep breath, almost sighing with relief.

"I believe our boss has spoken with you," he said.

"He has indeed."

She had to be careful in what she said. Telephone lines were not private although plans were in place to make them so. For the moment telephone lines were shared and anyone picking up a receiver at an inconvenient moment could listen in – and that was not even to mention the women working as telephonists who listened in when bored – it was best to be careful what one said.

"Why didn't you tell him that the plan is farcical?"

"One does not tell one's boss that he is foolish. One says, yes sir, no sir, three bags full sir." Perry said. "Did you not tell him that you doubted the efficiency of this idea?"

"I did," Krista said. "He reminded me that he is my boss and as such his word is law."

"Just so," Perry agreed. "But all that is not the purpose of my telephone call, darling."

"Oh?"

"Well, I thought we could escape for a few days." Perry lowered his voice. "I have the campervan. We could be together and private. What do you say?"

"That sounds wonderful." Krista tried to giggle but failed. "Do I need to bring anything?"

"I would love to say only yourself, darling, but I did wonder if you could take care of the supplies we'll need. I won't have time to stock the campervan. You are so talented in the kitchen." He could almost see her gritting her teeth. "Could you take care of stocking up, darling?"

"I would love to," Krista said with so much false sweetness that it sickened her.

"I'll pick you up tomorrow morning," Perry said. "I cannot wait to be with you, my love!" He almost laughed, imagining the fury on her face. "I hate to hang up the telephone, but I must if I am to be ready for the morning. Bye, bye."

"Goodbye, darling, drive carefully!" Krista had to struggle to replace the hand-piece of the telephone back in its place – gently. She turned to walk towards the kitchen, speaking aloud as she went. "I don't care what time it is. I am tempted to put some cognac in my coffee."

The kitchen was cold. She opened the door of the range, delighted to discover that someone – one of the Fagin women – had cleaned out the range and set the fire. She almost cried at the thoughtfulness. She was cold and miserable. She put a match to the crumpled paper in the range, watching the fire catch. She had to force herself to turn away from the flickering heat. She wanted coffee and thanks to her brother she could enjoy a pot without worry for her supplies. She began to fill the cafetiere.

"Perry wants me to stock the campervan." She was speaking aloud to herself to hide the loneliness of the empty cottage. She didn't want to turn on the wireless. She didn't feel she could cope with the almost constant barrage of bad news. "Well, I am going to take my cafetiere and coffee with me. I will include tea for Perry, of course. I'll make a list of what we will need to see us through the days and nights. Reggie said that Perry would have the equipment we might need, so I thankfully don't need to worry about that."

Krista checked on the fire in the range, put the coffee to percolate on the range top and left the kitchen. She went up the stairs, carrying her motorcycle helmet with her. She needed to change out of her uniform slacks and jumper. She intended to carry her clothes down to the kitchen and change there. She was alone and the heat from the range would be welcome. She hated to remove her leather jacket. She examined her clothing for muck. The roads had been particularly nasty today. She'd hang everything in the bathroom over the bath to allow the muck she'd picked up on her travels to dry.

Later that evening when she sat alone before the fire she'd lit in the living room, she thought about what she needed to do. The wireless played softly in the background. A selection of dance music from the Savoy Hotel ballroom. The music gave a lift to her spirits. She would have to examine the campervan. It had been well stocked for their travel to Europe but was it still? They needed dishes, cutlery and essentials. She had found two wooden boxes in the pantry and put them to one side. She could use them as packing cases. She had enough bread and milk for today and tomorrow but then she would have to purchase fresh.

When a waltz started playing on the wireless, she wished briefly for a romantic partner.

"There is no one stopping me dancing."

She pushed to her feet and, humming along with the music, in her stocking feet waltzed around the room in the arms of an imaginary beau.

*   *   *

"Good morning, Perry." Krista had waited until he'd parked the campervan at the verge in front of the cottage before opening the door. She wanted to keep the heat inside.

"Good morning!" Perry hurried up the garden path. He admired Mrs Fagin, but he has no desire to see her this morning. He and Krista had matters to discuss.

"Come inside quickly." Krista held the door open. "I have the kettle on."

"I'd love a mug of tea." Perry stepped inside and followed Krista down the hall to the kitchen.

"I cannot believe that I will be once more perched on top of a cliff!" Krista busied herself preparing a pot of tea. She already had a pot of coffee on the go. "If you knew how many days and nights I have spent on top of cliffs!" She and her roommates had spent months touring the southeast coast, searching out areas where a radio mast could be erected.

"We will be warm and comfortable. Captain Waters has placed his campervan at our disposal. You will not be hanging off the side of a cliff." He remembered the horror he had felt watching Krista and her fellow Wrens struggling through a storm to climb a sheer cliff-face.

"I still think the whole idea is ridiculous," Krista said. "How on earth are we supposed to stop anyone?"

"We have both been issued with Enfield No. 2 handguns," Perry said softly. "I have the guns and ammunition stored in the hidden storage space in the campervan."

"Oh." Krista didn't know what to say. She had been trained in the use of the handgun before she went to Europe but the thought of needing or indeed using such a thing on British soil didn't sit well with her.

"Master Sergeant Hemp was rightfully proud of your skill, Krista." Perry didn't think the cottage was the place to discuss arming a female. "We can speak of this later."

While Perry enjoyed his first mug of tea, Krista walked into the pantry. She had to put aside her concerns about their mission. She needed to prepare their food supplies. It would appear Perry and Captain Waters had taken care of ordnance.

She began to search the shelves of the pantry for something to fill the sandwiches she planned to make. She had stashed most of the goods her brother Philippe had left with her under her bed. Some of the smaller items were in the pantry and with a cry of pleasure she spied a tin of salmon.

"Perry, do you like caviar?" she called out, wondering if she could offload the item on him.

"Not particularly!" he called back.

"I hope you like salmon." She walked out of the pantry, tin of salmon in hand. "I'm going to hard-boil some eggs to take with us."

"Krista, have you forgotten we have a way of cooking in the campervan?"

"Yes, I know, Perry, but we don't know how long this adventure will take. If we are to park the campervan on top of a cliff, we will be unable to pop out for supplies. I prefer to be prepared. I want my cafetière and supply of coffee."

Perry stopped arguing and watched as she prepared what she considered essential supplies. She packed the items into wooden vegetable boxes she or Mrs Fagin must have picked up from the local greengrocer's. He looked at the wooden boxes and wondered when such things would be difficult to find. It seemed to him that so many familiar items were disappearing from everyday life.

"We need to talk about this mission, Perry, where no one can overhear what we are saying." Krista was cutting a loaf of bread thinly. "When Elaine and I were based on cliff tops listening in to ships' radios Elaine was convinced that anything we might say on the cliffs could be heard by those listening out to sea."

"It is certainly possible. It would depend on the equipment being used." Perry said.

"We won't be able to see a hand in front of our face when the sun goes down. It will be black as pitch. I have visions of both of us sitting staring out the window of the campervan into the darkness for days on end."

"What are you really worrying about?" Perry knew her well enough to know that she was not usually this negative.

"I don't know if I can stay awake all night." Krista kept her eyes on her hands. "We need to be alert at all times – that is exhausting in itself."

"The reason we are searching out a campsite this early is in order for us to take a nap." Perry said. "The powers that be believe that the ships take on passengers in the early hours of the morning. We are to listen and report what we might see and hear."

"Perry ..." Krista started.

He waited.

"I don't know if I can shoot someone."

"We don't know what we are facing. It is believed that the people being picked up along the coast are German spies. If we are forced to face off with some desperate person, we must protect ourselves. Someone trying to flee the country and report back to his superiors will not hesitate to shoot us."

"I'm sorry." Krista's hands were white-knuckled on the knife handle. "It is one thing to train and shoot at paper targets. Thinking about killing another human being is sickening."

"We are at war, Krista." Perry understood but they could not hesitate. "I need to know you have my back."

CHAPTER 13

The campervan was parked on a clifftop. The kettle had been boiled on the spirit stove, sandwiches were unwrapped and on a plate. Table and chairs unfolded.

"Elaine and I perched on the lip of this cliff for days." Krista was sitting on one of the folding chairs, an enamel mug of tea in hand.

"I have to get the radio antenna set up." Perry tucked into a cheese-and-tomato sandwich with relish. "If you'll make a show of hunting for sticks while I'm doing that, anyone that happens to see us will – hopefully – be thrown off the scent."

"I want to dry-fire my gun, Perry," Krista said. "I'd prefer live firing but that would be difficult to explain."

Perry waited until his mouth was clear to say, "It's an Enfield No. 2, Krista – you were trained on them."

"I'd still prefer to have some practice on it. No two guns fire alike as Master Sergeant Hemp told us time without number."

They drank the tea, ate sandwiches, and spoke about their mission in general terms. When the table and chairs had been folded, dishes washed and put away, Perry raised the antenna that had been disguised to look like part of the vehicle. Krista opened the door in the body of the camper and stepped outside. She wore a warm coat over her skirt and jumper. She wasn't wearing the pretty dress as advised by Rear Admiral Andrews – she was wearing a tweed skirt with kick pleats for easy movement.

"I'll gather some firewood, darling!" she called back gaily. "We want to be toasty warm!"

"There is a concert being broadcast from the Savoy on the wireless this evening." Perry stood in the open door of the campervan. "I'll light the fire as soon as I've powered up the generator. We can dine by candlelight while listening to music. Shall I open a bottle of wine, darling?"

"That would be lovely!" Krista called back.

She'd walked slowly around the clearing where they had parked the campervan. She began to wander further afield, through grassland sparsely dotted with trees, gathering sticks as she went. When she had checked out the area and gathered armloads of sticks, she stepped back into the campervan.

"Lock the door." Perry was standing by one of the panels that concealed a storage space. The campervan had been designed with espionage in mind. He began to remove the cover as soon as he heard the lock snick into place.

"Shall I draw the blinds, darling?" Krista stood ready to take the items he was removing from their hiding place.

"We could perhaps leave the blinds on the window facing the ocean open." Perry continued to remove radio parts, handgun, rifle and ammunition from the storage spaces. "I thought it would be romantic to watch the moon and stars over the sea." He waited until he had finished speaking to lift the panel and put it back in place. He didn't want to grunt while he was supposed to be whispering sweet nothings. "I'll get the fire started."

"I'll prepare something wonderful for us to eat."

While Perry tended to the fire, Krista stashed the holstered handguns and rifle in one of the storage spaces under the campervan benches. She assembled the crystal-powered radios before examining the campervan for the best place to set the foldaway table and chairs. They needed to see out of the window over the cliff to the sea but they must not be seen sitting with earphones on their heads.

They settled into a routine. It was difficult for two active people. The radio had to be manned. They took to sleeping in shifts. They loudly invented reasons to be outside. Each sought out hiding places – in case of necessity. They strolled hand in hand along the cliff. They had to give the semblance of romance.

On the fourth day of manning the radio, Perry shook Krista from a nap. He pressed the earphone to her without a word. On his knees he crawled to the window.

Krista listened with mounting horror. She began to crawl towards where he knelt in front of the window, binoculars pressed to his eyes. She was careful not to knot the wires of the earphones as she crawled – silently cursing the skirt she was wearing.

"We need help. There are six enemy agents nearby waiting for a submarine." Krista had her lips almost pressed to his ear. "Can you see anything?"

"Nothing out of the ordinary." Perry turned his head to whisper. They had become familiar with the sea traffic while keeping watch.

"Do we pack up and leave?" Krista wondered if they would be allowed to leave. They needed to notify headquarters.

"We cannot allow the information these men carry to leave the country. It is up to us to stop them. This is not the first time they've parked a submarine off this coastline." Perry was furious. "They are behaving as if they were in their own waters. This is madness."

Krista was listening to the ship-to-shore German conversation over her earphones, translating it into English for Perry's benefit. "They've encountered no true opposition when they invade countries. They were waved and kissed into Austria, for goodness' sake!"

"I'm surprised their agents are not brazen enough to be standing on the cliff waving," Perry bit out.

"Whoever is keeping watch believes that we are lovers. He is impressed by your stamina." She blushed at the comments coming through the earphones. "He is wondering about putting you out of commission and allowing his men to amuse themselves with me." Her stomach curled at the obscene comments.

"They don't think leaving bodies bleeding on a clifftop might point the finger of suspicion at this area? Are they really that sanguine about their superiority?"

"Yes," Krista snapped. "They have been taught to believe that they answer to no man." She wondered about the space available. "Perry, it's a submarine. How much space would they have on that thing for extra men?"

"Standing room only." Perry dropped the binoculars. "But it would not be a long trip. They can come up for air when out to sea then offload in German-occupied water." He looked down at her. "If we send a message now, while they are actively using their ship-to-shore radio equipment, they could well pick up our signal and be forced to react. If that happens, Krista, you cannot hesitate to fire."

"These men I *could* shoot." After listening to their disgusting dialogue, she'd have no hesitation protecting herself and Perry.

"We need to move to that trench we found." Perry's mind was spinning. "I covered it with a tarp and put water inside." They had found a dip in the land that was almost a trench while out strolling hand in hand. He had prepared it for their occupation.

"Would it not be better to stay with the campervan?" Even as she asked, Krista was preparing their haversacks.

"If someone got a lucky shot into the fuel supply it would be all over for us."

"Do we stroll out hand in hand or crawl out?" Krista asked.

"I know you brought your waterproof gear." Perry had seen her load it into the campervan. "We should crawl out."

They began to lock up the campervan, hiding away anything that might reveal their purpose. Krista changed into her waxed coat and slacks, glad she'd thought to throw them in at the last minute. She strapped her gun and holster around her waist.

"We'll leave the wireless playing." Perry opened the trapdoor in the floor of the campervan. "We'll crawl to the trench. Be sure you have everything you need to send and receive messages."

Krista had already double-checked that she had the radio, Morse code key and portable power pack.

"Send the message." Perry was out of the campervan.

Krista dropped the bags down onto the ground. She rapidly tapped out her message.

Darlings – stop – so many want to join us – stop – what should I feed them – stop – six extra – stop – such a bother – stop

She pushed the Morse code key back into its pack and dropped down below the campervan. She shoved her arms into the straps of the packs Perry held out for her and crawling forward they checked the area around them.

They reached the trench area safely. Krista wasted no time attaching the earpiece of the Morse code set to her ear. They loaded their pistols and

Perry's rifle and put boxes of ammunition close to hand. Perry took up position overlooking the campervan. Krista stationed herself at the rear of the trench to watch for any newcomers.

"They've heard the message. They're not sure where it was sent from." She stopped whispering when she heard loud voices and boots walking along the flattened ground that led to their camping area.

Two men appeared, laughing and talking, wearing heavy jackets, haversacks on their backs, hiking boots on their feet. They called out a friendly greeting when they neared the campervan.

"They have to be two of the six." Perry, rifle in hand, waited. "Their English is unaccented."

They watched one of the men knock on the campervan door. When there was no response the second man pulled a handgun from his pocket, pointing it at the campervan. "*We know that you are in there – come out!*"

"I don't believe this." Perry was astonished by this behaviour. They hadn't even waited before pulling a gun.

"*Kick the door in!*" the one with the gun barked.

"They truly expect no opposition." Perry gasped when they kicked open the door and began shooting into the interior. "First shots fired." He sighted down the rifle barrel and got off two shots, injuring both men before they could step into the campervan.

Shouting and running footsteps were heard. Krista, her gun in hand, waited. She knew the shooting range of her gun. She'd wait until they came in range. She fired two shots at the first man running towards the campervan, gun in hand. He grunted and fell but she didn't know how badly she had injured him. His companions approached more cautiously but they still did not seek cover. One man barked into a radio mouthpiece while he ran.

What happened next was terrifying. The submarine rose into the open. Its guns trained on the cliff face. The roar of the guns followed swiftly after their appearance.

"Get down!" Perry said. "The captain of that submarine has run mad. They are blind-firing live rounds. What do they imagine they can achieve with such bravado? He must imagine that flying shrapnel or exploding pieces of the cliff face will deter us. Which is sheer folly – they stand a chance of injuring their own people. It is sheer madness and do they really believe they can get away with firing on us in British waters?"

"These men must be important."

"Or the information they carry is important." Perry prayed that parts of the cliff did not explode upwards and fall on their hiding place.

"I have four behind us," Krista said. "One injured."

"I have two injured – I don't know how badly. They are lying down with their arms protecting their heads. They have enough sense not to make a target of themselves."

The orders were being issued with gunfire rapidity in fluent German. There was no attempt to hide what they were doing.

"Dear Lord!" Krista gasped. "Perry, shoot two of the campervan tires. They plan to use it to make their getaway."

Perry shot instantly.

"*I know you understand what I am saying!*" This was shouted in German as soon as the sound of bullets hitting the campervan tires rang out. "You are one man! You must protect your pretty companion. Throw down your gun and we will let you live."

A man stepped into view. Krista shot twice. She knew she hit the figure. He jerked and fell to the ground, screaming.

"*Ach so*, you are not an English gentleman." This in accented English. "Throw out your guns or I will have my ship destroy this cliff. You do not want your pretty lady to die, do you?"

"He is trying to trick us into answering." Krista said. "He is not sure where we are."

"*Heinz, do not give that order!*" One of the men lying in front of the campervan shouted in German.

"You must be ready to die for the Fatherland." They supposed it was Heinz who laughed. Two shots rang out and the men lying in front of the campervan jerked. Another two shots and they stopped moving.

"He shot his own men." Perry couldn't believe the evidence of his own eyes.

"They were injured. They would be a liability." Krista jerked when two more shots sounded. "I think he has just eliminated the two I injured. That was a handgun. To make those shots at the campervan count he must be close. Pass me your gun, Perry. If he is counting shots, he knows I have two bullets left in the barrel. He will be counting on me stopping to reload."

"Here!" Perry, without taking his eyes off the view in front of him swung the leather holster holding his handgun towards Krista.

"There you are!" The tarp over their heads was suddenly pulled back and a grinning face peered down at them. "Like rats in a hole!" He levelled a pistol towards the back of Perry's head, ignoring Krista.

It happened in an instant. Krista opened fire.

The sound of massive guns echoed over the water. Krista couldn't pay attention. She needed Perry's gun. She didn't have time to reload her own. There was still one man out there. She had Perry's gun in hand and cautiously raised her head over the lip of the trench. Where was the other man? The German? The man she just shot had no accent.

"*Nein!*" He stood over them, a grenade in hand.

"*Perry, hug the dirt!*" Krista shot, trying to stop him before he pulled the pin.

He pulled the pin of the grenade free and with an overarm throw sent it back in the direction he'd come from.

"*You will not have me, Englander!*" He grinned and shot himself in the head.

Krista threw herself out of the trench and crawled far enough away that she was free of the sight. She bent over and vomited everything she had eaten in the last week, tears flowed down her face.

"Here." Perry passed her a canteen. "Rinse your mouth. We need to check out the area."

"What was that noise?" Krista pushed herself to her feet. She sipped and spat.

"A British gunship arrived and fired on the submarine before it could sink under the waves."

"The German man threw a grenade in this direction." She pointed. "If I had to guess I believe he tried to destroy their campsite."

"Let's check it out."

Before they could move the sound of vehicles came from the road. There were shouts and the sound of booted feet.

"Our backup has arrived." Perry allowed himself to fall down.

"Now the questions begin." Krista sat beside him.

TO BE CONTINUED